CHRISTMAS
C L A S S I C S

CHRISTMAS
C L A S S I C S

A Festive Collection of Merry Masterpieces

Edited by Molly Cooper
Illustrated by Barbara Kiwak

Lowell House
C L A S S I C S

CONTEMPORARY BOOKS
Chicago

ISBN: 1-56565-490-0

Library of Congress Catalog: 96-2985

Publisher: Jack Artenstein
General Manager, Juvenile Division: Elizabeth Amos
Director of Publishing Services: Rena Copperman
Editor-and-Chief of Fiction, Juvenile Division: Barbara Schoichet
Managing Editor, Juvenile Division: Lindsey Hay
Art Director: Lisa-Theresa Lenthall

Lowell House books can be purchased at special discounts
when ordered in bulk for premiums and special sales.
Contact Department JH at the following address:

Lowell House Juvenile
2029 Century Park East, Suite 3290
Los Angeles, CA 90067

Manufactured in the United States of America

10 9 8 7 6 5 4 3 2 1

CONTENTS

CHRISTMAS CLASSICS
INTRODUCTION

Dear Reader:

To many people, Christmas is the most special day of the year. After all the hustle and bustle of putting up decorations, going to parties, frantically shopping for presents, generously giving gifts, and graciously receiving them, it all comes down to this—Christmas is a time of year we think of others. We feel a little bit kinder, a little bit more optimistic, and a little bit happier just to be alive, and we want others to feel that way, too.

Santa Claus, that jolly, plump, white-bearded, red-suited fellow, of course, is one of the main figures that comes to mind during the Christmas season. But did you know that originally there was a *real* man named St. Nicholas? The story goes that while roaming about his village one day, this kind gentleman heard of a poor merchant who did not have enough money to provide dowries for his three daughters. St. Nicholas, a merchant himself, understood the poor fellow's predicament and felt very bad for the man and his family.

One evening, St. Nicholas crept over to the merchant's house and tossed three bags of gold into the window—one for the dowries of each of the merchant's daughters. Imagine the family's surprise when they awoke the next morning!

Determined to find out who his benefactor was, the poor merchant eventually discovered that it was indeed none other than St. Nicholas. However, being a modest man, St. Nicholas made the merchant swear never to tell anyone about his good deed.

Well, obviously the merchant must have had a hard time keeping the secret, for St. Nicholas's reputation for spreading cheer and the spirit of goodwill is very much alive today.

The wonderful stories, excerpts, and poems in CHRISTMAS CLASSICS all display the delight and joy of this most festive of holidays. Each is a beautiful gift in itself, and will surely remind everyone just how special this holiday is and how important it is to honor the true meaning of Christmas.

And now, as you are about to read this treasury of tales, keep in mind the words of one of the master storytellers represented in this book, Charles Dickens. "I will honor Christmas in my heart," said the famous author of *A Christmas Carol*, "and try to keep it all the year."

THE NIGHT BEFORE CHRISTMAS

by Clement C. Moore

The beloved Christmas classic, "A Visit from St. Nicholas," known to most as "The Night Before Christmas," was the sole work which brought scholar Clement Clarke Moore literary fame. Published anonymously a year after it was written in 1822, the poem became a huge success, appearing in newspapers, school readers, and anthologies.

Born in New York on July 15, 1779, Moore was tutored at home until he entered Columbia College where he graduated at the top of his class in 1798. In 1801 he received his masters from Columbia, and in 1829 he earned a law degree. During this time he met Catherine Elizabeth Taylor, whom he married in 1813, and with whom he eventually had nine children. Moore continued his scholarly achievements at the General Theological Seminary, where he was a professor of Oriental and Greek literature until his retirement in 1850. He then purchased a home in Newport, Rhode Island where he remained until his death on July 10, 1863.

Although Moore wrote more than poetry, including criticism, French translations, and an historical biography, his famous poem wasn't even printed under his own name until 1844 when he published a collection called Poems. Because Moore had written the poem for his children, six of whom were born before 1822, he had no intention of publishing it. The story goes that a houseguest, Harriet Butler, heard the poem and sent it to the editor of the Sentinel. The editor, Orville L. Holley, was delighted with the piece, and it has since been republished numerous times, and has become a classic throughout the world.

'Twas the night before Christmas, when all though the house
Not a creature was stirring, not even a mouse;
The stockings were hung by the chimney with care,
In hopes that ST. NICHOLAS soon would be there;

The children were nestled all snug in their beds,
While visions of sugar-plums danced through their heads;
And Mamma in her 'kerchief, and I in my cap,
Had just settled down for a long winter's nap,—

When out on the lawn there arose such a clatter,
I sprang from my bed to see what was the matter;
Away to the window I flew like a flash,
Tore open the shutters and threw up the sash.

The moon on the breast of the new-fallen snow
Gave the lustre of midday to objects below;
When, what to my wondering eyes should appear,
But a miniature sleigh, and eight tiny reindeer,

With a little old driver, so lively and quick,
I knew in a moment it must be SAINT NICK.
More rapid than eagles his coursers they came,
And he whistled, and shouted, and called them by name:

"Now, *Dasher!* now, *Dancer!* now, *Prancer* and *Vixen!*
On, *Comet!* on, *Cupid!* on, *Donder* and *Blitzen!*
To the top of the porch! to the top of the wall!
Now, dash away! dash away! dash away all!"

As dry leaves that before the wild hurricane fly,
When they meet with an obstacle, mount to the sky,
So up to the house-top the coursers they flew,
With a sleigh full of toys—and ST. NICHOLAS too!

And then, in a twinkling, I heard on the roof,
The prancing and pawing of each little hoof.
As I drew in my head, and was turning around,
Down the chimney ST. NICHOLAS came with a bound.

He was dressed all in fur, from his head to his foot,
And his clothes were all tarnished with ashes and soot!
A bundle of toys he had flung on his back,
And he looked like a peddler just opening his pack;

His eyes—how they twinkled! his dimples, how merry!
His cheeks were like roses, his nose like a cherry!
His droll little mouth was drawn up like a bow,
And the beard of his chin was as white as the snow.

The stump of his pipe he held tight in his teeth,
And the smoke, it encircled his head like a wreath.
He had a broad face, and a little round belly,
That shook, when he laugh'd, like a bowlful of jelly.

He was chubby and plump; a right jolly old elf;
And I laughed, when I saw him, in spite of myself.
A wink of his eye, and a twist of his head,
Soon gave me to know I had nothing to dread.

He spoke not a word, but went straight to his work,
And filled all the stockings—then turned with a jerk,
And laying his finger aside of his nose,
And giving a nod, up the chimney he rose.

He sprang to his sleigh, to his team gave a whistle,
And away they all flew, like the down off a thistle.
But I heard him exclaim, ere he drove out of sight,
"Happy Christmas to all! and to all a good night!"

Yes, Virginia, there is a Santa Claus. . . .
Thank God! he lives, and he lives forever.
A thousand years from now, Virginia, nay ten times ten
thousand years from now, he will continue to make glad
the heart of childhood.

*Written by Francis Pharcellus Church, as an editorial response
to a letter from eight-year-old Virginia O'Hanlon: "Please tell
me the truth; is there a Santa Claus?"*

New York Sun [September 21, 1897]

A MERRY CHRISTMAS
(AN EXCERPT FROM *LITTLE WOMEN*)

by Louisa May Alcott

Born on November 29, 1832, in Germantown, Pennsylvania, Louisa May Alcott is known for her heartwarming depictions of family life in New England. Her father, Amos Bronson Alcott, was a philosopher, and was friends with many leading intellectuals of the time. Therefore, Louisa was influenced by such famous thinkers as Ralph Waldo Emerson, Henry David Thoreau, and Nathaniel Hawthorne. Her father, however, proved financially unstable, and Louisa resolved to provide for the family at the early age of twelve.

Beginning her writing career in her late teens and early twenties, Alcott first began submitting short stories to magazines such as the Saturday Evening Gazette and Atlantic Monthly. In 1855 she published a collection of fairy tales called Flower Fables. But because the book brought her little financial success, Alcott turned to hack writing, or more commercial writing designed to appeal to a wider audience. While this formula type of writing did allow Alcott to support her family, she herself was unsatisfied and longed to do something more substantial with her life.

To that end, the soon-to-be-famous author decided to become a nurse, and in December of 1862, she became an army nurse caring for wounded Civil War soldiers. Later she compiled the letters she wrote to her family from her Washington, D.C. post and published them as a book entitled, Hospital Sketches, which proved to be her first literary success.

When the war was over, Alcott accepted the editor's position at Merry's Museum, a children's magazine. Finally, in January 1868, she wrote a short story about four girls and their devoted mother that, just six weeks later, would blossom into her most famous full-length novel, Little Women. Printed in September 1868, the book was an overnight success. A few months later, Alcott wrote the sequel, Little Women, Part Second, which also enjoyed enormous popularity.

Although she never married, Alcott led a full life devoted to her family and her work. Unfortunately, however, while serving as a nurse, she contracted typhoid fever. Although cured, Alcott never quite felt well again, and toward the end of her life, her health quickly deteriorated. On March 6, 1888, the author died in her sleep—just two days after her father's death.

In this excerpt of Little Women, the four March girls feel the effect of a very poor Christmas, but are trying to make the best of it. They have managed to buy Christmas presents for their mother, but she is nowhere to be found. Imagine their surprise and delight when they find out where she is, and how it helps them discover the true meaning of Christmas.

"Christmas won't be Christmas without any presents," grumbled Jo, lying on the rug.

"It's so dreadful to be poor!" sighed Meg, looking down at her old dress.

"I don't think it's fair for some girls to have lots of pretty things, and other girls nothing at all," added little Amy, with an injured sniff.

"We've got Father and Mother, and each other, anyhow," said Beth, contentedly, from her corner.

The four young faces on which the firelight shone brightened at the cheerful words, but darkened again as Jo said sadly, "We haven't got Father, and shall not have him for a long time." She didn't say "perhaps never," but each silently added it, thinking of Father far away.

Nobody spoke for a minute; then Meg said in an altered tone, "You know the reason Mother proposed not having any presents this Christmas was because it's going to be a hard winter for every one; and she thinks we ought not to spend any money for pleasure, when our men are suffering so in the army. We can't do much, but we can make our little sacrifices, and ought to do it gladly. But I am afraid I don't." Meg shook her head, as she thought regretfully of all the pretty things she wanted.

"But I don't think the little we should spend would do any good. We've each got a dollar, and the army wouldn't be much helped by our giving that. I agree not to expect anything from mother or you, but I do want to buy *Undine and Sintram* for myself; I've wanted it so long," said Jo, who was a bookworm.

"I planned to spend mine on new music," said Beth, with a little sigh.

"I shall get a nice box of Faber's drawing pencils; I really need them," said Amy, decidedly.

"Mother didn't say anything about our money, and she won't wish us to give up everything. Let's each buy what we want, and have a little fun; I'm sure we grub hard enough to earn it," cried Jo, examining the heels of her boots in a gentlemanly manner.

"I know *I* do—teaching those dreadful children nearly all day, when I'm longing to enjoy myself at home," began Meg, in the complaining tone again.

"You don't have half such a hard time as I do," said Jo. "How would you like to be shut up for hours with a nervous, fussy old lady, who keeps you trotting, is never satisfied, and worries you till you're ready to fly out of the window or box her ears?"

"It's naughty to fret—but I do think washing dishes and keeping things tidy is the worst work in the world. It makes me cross; and my hands get so stiff, I can't practice good a bit." And Beth looked at her rough hands with a sigh that any one could hear that time.

"I don't believe any of you suffer as I do," cried Amy; "for you don't have to go to school with impertinent girls, who plague you if you don't know your lessons, and laugh at your dresses, and label your father if he isn't rich, and insult you when your nose isn't nice."

"If you mean *libel* I'd say so, and not talk about *labels*, as if Pa was a pickle-bottle," advised Jo, laughing.

"I know what I mean, and you needn't be 'statirical' about it. It's proper to use good words, and improve your *vocabilary*," returned Amy, with dignity.

"Don't peck at one another, children," said Meg.

It was a comfortable old room, though the carpet was faded and the furniture very plain, for a good picture or two hung on the walls, books filled the recesses, chrysanthemums and Christmas roses bloomed in the windows, and a pleasant atmosphere of home peace pervaded it.

Margaret, the eldest of the four, was sixteen, and very pretty. Fifteen-year-old Jo was tall, thin, and brown, and reminded one of a colt; for she never seemed to know what to do with her long limbs, which were very much in her way. Elizabeth—or Beth, as every one called her—was a rosy, smooth-haired, bright-eyed girl of thirteen. Amy, though the youngest, was a most important person, in her own opinion at least.

The clock struck six; and, having swept up the hearth, Beth put a pair of slippers down to warm. Somehow the sight of the old shoes had a good effect upon the girls, for Mother was coming, and every one brightened to welcome her.

"They are worn out; Marmee must have a new pair."

"I thought I'd get her some with my dollar," said Beth.

"No, I shall!" cried Amy.

"I'm the oldest," began Meg, but Jo cut in with a decided—"I'm the man of the family, now that Papa is away, and I shall provide the slippers, for he told me to take special care of Mother while he was gone."

"I'll tell you what," said Beth; "let's each get her something for Christmas, and not get anything for ourselves."

"That's like you, dear! What will we get?" exclaimed Jo.

Every one thought soberly for a minute; then Meg announced, as if the idea was suggested by the sight of her own pretty hands, "I shall give her a nice pair of gloves."

"Army shoes, best to be had," cried Jo.

"Some handkerchiefs, all hemmed," said Beth.

"I'll get a little bottle of Cologne; she likes it, and it won't cost much, so I'll have some left to buy something for me," added Amy.

"How will we give the things?" asked Meg.

"Put 'em on the table, and bring her in and see her open the bundles," answered Jo.

"Well, dearies, how have you got on today?" said a cherry voice at the door. "There was so much to do, getting the boxes ready to go tomorrow, that I didn't come home to dinner. Has any one called, Beth? How is your cold, Meg? Jo, you look tired to death. Come and kiss me, baby."

While making these maternal inquiries Mrs. March got her wet things off, her hot slippers on, and sitting down in the easy chair, drew Amy to her lap, preparing to enjoy the happiest hour of her busy day. The girls flew about, trying to make things comfortable, each in her own way. Meg arranged the tea table; Jo brought wood and set chairs, dropping, overturning, and clattering everything she touched; Beth trotted to and fro between parlor and kitchen, quiet and busy; while Amy gave directions to every one, as she sat with her hands folded.

As they gathered about the table, Mrs. March said, with a particularly happy face, "I've got a treat for you after supper."

A quick, bright smile went round like a streak of sunshine. Beth clapped her hands, regardless of the hot biscuit she held, and Jo tossed up her napkin, crying, "A letter! A letter! Three cheers for Father!"

"Yes, a nice long letter. He is well, and thinks he shall get through the cold season better than we feared. He sends all sorts of loving wishes for Christmas, and an especial message to our girls," said Mrs. March, patting her pocket as if she had got a treasure there.

"Hurry up, and get done. Don't primp over your plate, Amy," cried Jo, choking in her tea, and dropping her bread, butter side down, on the carpet, in her haste to get at the treat.

Beth ate no more, but crept away, to sit in her shadowy corner and brood over the delight to come.

"I think it was so splendid of Father to go as a chaplain when he was too old to be drafted, and not strong enough for a soldier," said Meg, warmly.

"When will he come home, Marmee?" asked Beth, with a little quiver in her voice.

"Not for many months, dear, unless he is sick. He will stay and do his work faithfully as long as he can, and we won't ask for him back a minute sooner than he can be spared. Now come and hear the letter."

They all drew to the fire, Mother in the big chair with Beth at her feet, Meg and Amy perched on either arm of the chair, and Jo leaning on the back, where no one would see any sign of emotion if the letter should be touching.

Very few letters were written in those hard times that were not touching, especially those which fathers sent home. In this one little was said of the hardships endured, the dangers faced, or the homesickness conquered; it was a cheerful, hopeful letter, full of lively descriptions of camp life, and only at the end did the writer's heart overflow with fatherly love and longing for the little girls at home.

"Give them all my dear love and a kiss. Tell them I think of them by day, pray for them by night, and find my best comfort in their affection at all times. A year seems very long to wait before I see them, but remind them that while we wait we may all work, so that these hard days need not be wasted. I know they will remember all I said to them, that they will be loving children to you, will do their duty faithfully, fight their bosom enemies bravely, and conquer themselves so beautifully, that when I come back to them I may be fonder and prouder than ever of my little women."

Everybody sniffed when they came to that part; Jo wasn't ashamed of the great tear that dropped off the end of her nose, and Amy never minded the rumpling of her curls as she hid her face on her mother's shoulder and sobbed out, "I *am* a selfish pig! but I'll truly try to be better, so he mayn't be disappointed in me by and by."

"We all will!" cried Meg. "I think too much of my looks, and hate to work, but won't any more, if I can help it."

"I'll try to be what he loves to call me, 'a little woman,' and not be rough and wild; but do my duty here instead of wanting to be somewhere else," said Jo, thinking that keeping her temper at home was a much harder task than facing a rebel or two down South.

Beth said nothing, but wiped away her tears with the blue army-sock, and began to knit with all her might, losing no time in doing the duty that lay nearest her, while she resolved in her quiet little soul to be all that Father hoped to find when the year brought round the happy coming home.

Jo was the first to wake in the gray dawn of Christmas morning. No stockings hung at the fireplace, and for a moment she felt as much disappointed as she did long ago, when her little sock fell down because it was so crammed with goodies. Then she remembered her mother's promise, and slipping her hand under her pillow, drew out a little crimson-covered book.

She knew it very well, for it was that beautiful old story of the best life ever lived, and Jo felt that it was a true guide-book for any pilgrim going the long journey. She woke Meg with a "Merry Christmas," and bade her see what was under her pillow. A green-covered book appeared, with the same picture inside, and a few words written by their mother, which made their one present very precious in their eyes. Presently Beth and Amy woke, to rummage and find their little books also—one dove-colored, the other blue; and all sat looking at and talking about them, while the East grew rosy with the coming day.

"Girls," said Meg, seriously, looking from the tumbled head beside her to the two little night-capped ones in the room beyond, "Mother wants us to read and love and mind these books, and we must begin at once. We used to be faithful about it; but since Father went away, and all this war trouble unsettled us, we have neglected many things. You can do as you please; but I shall keep my book on the table here, and read a little every morning as soon as I wake, for I know it will do me good, and help me through the day."

Then she opened her new book and began to read. Jo put her arm around her, and, leaning cheek to cheek, read also, with the quiet expression so seldom seen on her restless face.

"How good Meg is! Come, Amy, let's do as they do. I'll help you with the hard words, and they'll explain things if we don't understand," whispered Beth, very much impressed by the pretty books and her sister's example.

"I'm glad mine is blue," said Amy; and then the rooms were very still while the pages were softly turned, and the winter sunshine crept in to touch the bright heads and serious faces with a Christmas greeting.

"Where is Mother?" asked Meg, as she and Jo ran down to thank her for their gifts, half an hour later.

"Goodness only knows. Some poor creeter come a-beggin', and your ma went off to see what was needed. There never was such a woman for givin' away vittles and clothes," replied Hannah, who had lived with the family since Meg was born, and was considered more a friend than a servant.

"She will be back soon, I guess; so do your cakes, and have everything ready," said Meg, looking over the presents which were in a basket under the sofa, ready to be produced at the proper time. "Why, where is Amy's bottle of Cologne?" she added, as the little flask did not appear.

"She took it out a minute ago, and went off with it to put a ribbon on it, or some such notion," replied Jo, dancing about the room to take the stiffness off the new army-slippers.

"How nice my handkerchiefs look, don't they? Hannah washed and ironed them for me, and I marked them all myself," said Beth, looking proudly at the somewhat uneven letters which had cost her such labor.

"Bless the child, she's gone and put 'Mother' on them instead of 'M. March'; how funny!" cried Jo, taking up one.

"Isn't it right? I thought it was better to do it so, because Meg's initials are 'M.M.,' and I don't want any one to use these but Marmee," said Beth, looking troubled.

"It's all right, dear, and a very pretty idea; quite sensible, too, for no one can ever mistake now. It will please her very much," said Meg, with a frown for Jo, and a smile for Beth.

"There's Mother; hide the basket, quick!" cried Jo, as a door slammed, and steps sounded in the hall.

Amy came in hastily, and looked rather abashed when she saw her sisters all waiting for her.

"Where have you been, and what are you hiding behind you?" asked Meg, surprised to see, by her hood and cloak, that lazy Amy had been out so early.

"Don't laugh at me, Jo, I didn't mean any one should know till the time came. I only meant to change the little bottle for a big one, and I gave *all* my money to get it, and I'm truly trying not to be selfish any more."

As she spoke, Amy showed the handsome flask which replaced the cheap one; and looked so earnest in her little effort to forget herself, that Meg hugged her on the spot, and Jo pronounced her "a trump," while Beth ran to the window, and picked her finest rose to ornament the stately bottle.

"You see, I felt ashamed of my present, after reading and talking about being good this morning, so I ran round the corner and changed it the minute I was up; and I'm glad, for mine is the handsomest now."

Another bang of the street-door sent the basket under the sofa, and the girls to the table eager for breakfast.

"Merry Christmas, Marmee! Lots of them! Thank you for our books; we read some, and mean to every day," they cried, in chorus.

"Merry Christmas, little daughters! I'm glad you began at once, and hope you will keep on. But I want to say one word before we sit down. Not far away from here lies a poor woman with a little new-born baby. Six children are huddled into one bed to keep from freezing, for they have no fire. There is nothing to eat over there; and the oldest boy came to tell me they were suffering hunger and cold. My girls, will you give them your breakfast as a Christmas present?"

They were all hungry, having waited nearly an hour, and for a minute no one spoke; only a minute, for Jo exclaimed impetuously, "I'm so glad you came before we began!"

"May I go and help carry the things to the poor little children?" asked Beth, eagerly.

"*I* shall take the cream and the muffins," added Amy, heroically giving up the articles she most liked.

Meg was already covering the buckwheats, and piling the bread into one big plate.

"I thought you'd do it," said Mrs. March, smiling as if satisfied. "You shall all go and help me, and when we come back we will have bread and milk for breakfast, and make it up at dinner-time."

They were soon ready, and the procession set out. Fortunately it was early, and they went through back streets, so few saw them, and no one laughed at the funny party.

A bare, miserable room it was, with broken windows, no fire, ragged bedclothes, a sick mother, wailing baby, and a group of pale, hungry children cuddled under one old quilt, trying to keep warm. How the big eyes stared, and the blue lips smiled, as the girls went in!

"*Ach, mein Gott!* It is good angels come to us!" cried the poor woman, crying for joy.

"Funny angels in hoods and mittens," said Jo, and set them laughing.

In a few minutes it really did seem as if kind spirits had been at work there. Hannah, who had carried wood, made a fire, and stopped up the broken panes with old hats, and her own shawl. Mrs. March gave the mother tea and gruel, and comforted her with promises of help, while she dressed the little baby as tenderly as if it had been her own. The girls, meantime, spread the table, set the children round the fire, and fed them like so many hungry birds; laughing, talking, and trying to understand the broken English.

"*Das ist gut! Die angel-kinder!*" cried the poor things, as they ate, and warmed their purple hands at the comfortable blaze. The girls had never been called angel children before, and thought it very agreeable. That was a very happy breakfast, though they didn't get any of it; and when they went away, leaving comfort behind, I think there were not in all the city four merrier people than the hungry little girls who gave away their breakfasts, and contented themselves with bread and milk on Christmas morning.

"That's loving our neighbor better than ourselves, and I like it," said Meg, as they set out their presents, while their mother was upstairs collecting clothes for the poor Hummels.

Not a very splendid show, but there was a great deal of love done up in the few little bundles; and the tall vase of red roses, white chrysanthemums, and trailing vines, which stood in the middle, gave quite an elegant air to the table.

"She's coming! strike up, Beth, open the door, Amy. Three cheers for Marmee!" cried Jo, prancing about, while Meg went to conduct Mother to the seat of honor.

Beth played her gayest march, Amy threw open the door, and Meg enacted escort with great dignity. Mrs. March was both surprised and touched; and smiled with her eyes full as she examined her presents, and read the little notes which accompanied them. The slippers went on at once, a new handkerchief was slipped into her pocket, well scented with

Amy's Cologne, the rose was fastened in her bosom, and the nice gloves were pronounced "a perfect fit."

There was a good deal of laughing, and kissing, and explaining, in the simple, loving fashion which makes these home festivals so pleasant at the time and so sweet to remember long afterward.

Beth nestled up to her mother, and whispered softly, "I'm afraid Father isn't having such a merry Christmas as we are."

God rest you merry, gentlemen,
Let nothing you dismay:
Remember Christ our Savior,
Was born on Christmas Day.

—ANONYMOUS CAROL

THE FIR TREE

by Hans Christian Andersen

From the very beginning, Hans Christian Andersen was bent on being famous. Born on April 2, 1805, in Odense, Denmark, his success remains a remarkable achievement not only as a tribute to his writing talents, but because he was the first Danish author to emerge from the working class. His father, a shoemaker, and his mother, a washerwoman, planned for young Andersen to become an apprentice to a tailor when he was fourteen. But the boy wanted a life of adventure and had other plans. After convincing his parents to let him choose his own path, Andersen set off for Copenhagen where he lived for three years trying to become a singer, dancer, and actor. He had no luck.

Fortunately, however, when Andersen was seventeen, a prominent government official arranged for him to continue his neglected studies, and in 1828, Andersen passed his university examinations by writing his first prose narrative, a satirical fantasy. After this success, Andersen's career as an author had begun. In 1835 he completed his first novel, The Improvisatore, and a small book of fairy tales, which went virtually unnoticed.

Although Andersen tried his hand at all sorts of writing, including drama, poetry, and travel books, his fairy tales are what made him one of the most beloved authors of his day. Retelling folk tales he heard as a child as well as creating original stories, Andersen believed that fairy tales were the "universal poetry" and would become the poetic form of the future. Although his prediction did not come true, his unique talent made him a quick success.

Andersen never married, and spent most of his life as a guest in the homes of wealthy country Danes. He loved to travel, and spent much of his time acquainting himself with prominent European authors, including the English novelist, Charles Dickens. After completing an autobiography, five novels, and 168 delightful and intriguing stories, including such favorites as "The Ugly Duckling," "The Princess and the Pea," and "The Little Mermaid," Andersen died on August 4, 1875.

In "The Fir Tree," a brother and sister aid a lost child who has come to their cottage for help. Imagine their surprise when they discover the child is not who he seems to be, but rather a blessing in disguise.

Most children have seen a Christmas tree, and many know that the pretty and pleasant custom of hanging gifts on its boughs comes from Germany; but perhaps few have heard or read the story that is told to little German children, respecting the origin of this custom. The story is called "The Little Stranger," and runs thus:

In a small cottage on the borders of a forest lived a poor laborer, who gained a scanty living by cutting wood. He had a wife and two children who helped him in his work. The boy's name was Valentine, and the girl was called Mary. They were obedient, good children, and a great comfort to their parents. One winter evening, this happy little family were sitting quietly round the hearth, the snow and the wind raging outside, while they ate their supper of dry bread, when a gentle tap was heard on the window, and a childish voice cried from without; "Oh, let me in, pray! I am a poor child, with nothing to eat, and no home to go to, and I shall die of cold and hunger unless you let me in."

Valentine and Mary jumped up from the table and ran to open the door, saying: "Come in, poor little child! We have not much to give you, but whatever we have we will share."

The stranger-child came in and warmed his frozen hands and feet at the fire, and the children gave him the best they had to eat, saying: "You must be tired, too, poor child! Lie down on our bed; we can sleep on the bench for one night."

Then said the little stranger-child: "Thank God for all your kindness to me!"

So they took their little guest into their sleeping-room, laid him on the bed, covered him over, and said to each other: "How thankful we ought to be! We have warm rooms and a cozy bed, while this poor child has only heaven for his roof and the cold earth for his sleeping-place."

When their father and mother went to bed, Mary and Valentine lay quite contentedly on the bench near the fire, saying, before they fell asleep: "The stranger-child will be so happy tonight in his warm bed!"

These kind children had not slept many hours before Mary awoke, and softly whispered to her brother: "Valentine, dear, wake, and listen to the sweet music under the window."

Then Valentine rubbed his eyes and listened. It was sweet music indeed, and sounded like beautiful voices singing to the tones of a harp:

"Oh holy Child, we great thee! bringing
Sweet strains of harp to aid our singing.
"Thou, holy Child, in peace art sleeping,
While we our watch without are keeping.
"Blest be the house wherein thou liest,
Happiest on earth, to heaven the nighest."

The children listened, while a solemn joy filled their hearts; then they stepped softly to the window to see who might be without.

In the east was a streak of rosy dawn, and in its light they saw a group of children standing before the house, clothed in silver garments, holding golden harps in their hands. Amazed at this sight, the children were still gazing out of the window, when a light tap caused them to turn around. There stood the stranger-child before them clad in a golden dress, with a gleaming radiance round his curling hair. "I am the little Christ-child," he said, "who wanders through the world bringing peace and happiness to good children. You took me in and cared for me when you thought me a poor child, and now you shall have my blessing for what you have done."

A fir tree grew near the house; and from this he broke a twig, which he planted in the ground, saying: "This twig shall become a tree, and shall bring forth fruit year by year for you."

No sooner had he done this than he vanished, and with him the little choir of angels. But the fir-branch grew and

became a Christmas tree, and on its branches hung golden apples and silver nuts every Christmas-tide.

Such is the story told to German children concerning their beautiful Christmas trees, though we know that the real little Christ-child can never be wandering, cold and homeless, again in our world, inasmuch as he is safe in heaven by his Father's side; yet we may gather from this story the same truth which the Bible plainly tells us—that anyone who helps a Christian child in distress, it will be counted unto him as if he had indeed done it unto Christ himself. "Inasmuch as ye have done it unto the least of these, my brethren, ye have done it unto me."

DULCE DOMUM
(AN EXCERPT FROM *THE WIND IN THE WILLOWS*)

by Kenneth Grahame

It is ironic that a man who hardly got to enjoy his own childhood would later be remembered by the literary world for his wonderful insight into a child's perception of things. But that is exactly what happened to Kenneth Grahame, who later penned one of the greatest childhood classics ever written, The Wind in the Willows.

Born on March 8, 1859, in Edinburgh, Scotland, Grahame lost his mother to scarlet fever when he was only five years old, and in essence lost his father as well when the grieving man left the boy with his grandmother to be raised. Later, when Grahame had just finished his basic schooling, he was forced to clerk for his uncle in a bank instead of continuing his education. Though Grahame stayed in banking until 1907, he also began his writing career in 1890 by publishing a few short works in a number of magazines and journals.

Later, in 1893, Grahame collected his tales and essays and published them as a book entitled, Pagan Papers, *but the collection proved to be unsuccessful. Just two years later, however,*

Grahame published his next work, The Golden Age, a lively novel about imaginative orphans who lived with dull, uncaring relatives, and he finally gained widespread acclaim from both the general public and critics alike.

In 1899 the now-famous author married Elspeth Thomson. Their son, Alistair, born the following year, was nearly blind, and Grahame began to tell the boy delightful bedtime stories filled with lovable talking animals. Eventually, in 1907, the world at large would come to know Grahame's imaginative creations such as Mr. Toad, Mole, and Rat, when they became the main characters in his most famous work, The Wind in the Willows. Unfortunately, however, over the next twenty-five years Grahame wrote little else, and he died of a brain hemorrhage in 1932.

In "Dulce Domum," which means "sweet house," Mole and Rat search for a fire and a hearty supper in the midst of an upcoming snowstorm. After peeking in on humans, who are having a most enviable warm and cozy Christmas, the furry pair trudge onward, unaware that they are in for a very special Christmas of their own.

The sheep ran huddling together against the hurdles, blowing out thin nostrils and stamping with delicate fore-feet, their heads thrown back and a light steam rising from the crowded sheep-pen into the frosty air, as the two animals hastened by in high spirits, with much chatter and laughter. They were returning across country after a long day's outing with Otter, hunting and exploring on the wide uplands where certain streams tributary to their own river had their first small beginnings; and the shades of the short winter day were closing in on them, and they still had some distance to go.

Plodding at random across the plough, they had heard the sheep and had made for them; and now, leading from the sheep-pen, they found a beaten track that made walking a lighter business, and responded, moreover, to that small inquiring something which all animals carry inside them, saying unmistakably, "Yes, quite right; this leads home!"

"It looks as if we were coming to a village," said the Mole somewhat dubiously, slackening his pace, as the track, that had in time become a path and then had developed into a lane, now handed them over to the charge of a well-metalled road. The animals did not hold with villages, and their own highways, thickly frequented as they were, took an independent course, regardless of church, post office, or public-house.

"Oh, never mind!" said the Rat. "At this season of the year they're all safe indoors by this time, sitting round the fire; men, women, and children, dogs and cats and all. We shall slip through all right, without any bother or unpleasantness, and we can have a look at them through their windows if you like, and see what they're doing."

The rapid nightfall of mid-December had quite beset the little village as they approached it on soft feet over a first thin fall of powdery snow. Little was visible but squares of a dusky orange-red on either side of the street, where the firelight or lamplight of each cottage overflowed through the casements into the dark world without. Most of the low latticed windows were innocent of blinds, and to the lookers-in from outside, the inmates, gathered round the tea-table, absorbed in handiwork, or talking with laughter or gesture, had each that happy grace which is the last thing the skilled actor shall capture—the natural grace which goes with perfect unconsciousness of observation. Moving at will from one theatre to another, the two spectators, so far from home themselves, had something of wistfulness in their eyes as they watched a cat being stroked, a sleepy child picked up and huddled off to bed, or a tired man stretch and knock out his pipe on the end of a smoldering log.

But it was from one little window, with its blind drawn down, a mere blank transparency on the night, that the sense of home and the little curtained world within walls—the larger stressful world of outside Nature shut out and forgotten—most pulsated. Close against the white blind hung a bird-cage, clearly silhouetted, every wire, perch, and appurtenance distinct and recognizable, even to yesterday's dull-edged lump of sugar. On the middle perch the fluffy occupant, head tucked well into feathers, seemed so near to them as to be easily stroked, had they tried; even the delicate tips of his plumped-out plumage penciled plainly on the illuminated screen.

As they looked, the sleepy little fellow stirred uneasily, woke, shook himself, and raised his head. They could see the gape of his tiny beak as he yawned in a bored sort of way, looked round, and then settled his head into his back again, while the ruffled feathers gradually subsided into perfect stillness. Then a gust of bitter wind took them in the back of the neck, a small sting of frozen sleet on the skin woke them as from a dream, and they knew their toes to be cold and their legs tired, and their own home distant a weary way.

Once beyond the village, where the cottages ceased abruptly, on either side of the road they could smell through the darkness the friendly fields again; and they braced themselves for the last long stretch, the home stretch, the stretch that we know is bound to end, some time, in the rattle of the door-latch, the sudden firelight, and the sight of familiar things greeting us as long-absent travelers from far oversea. They plodded along steadily and silently, each of them thinking his own thoughts. The Mole's ran a good deal on supper, as it was pitch-dark, and it was all a strange country to him as far as he knew, and he was following obediently in the wake of the Rat, leaving the guidance entirely to him. As for the Rat, he was walking a little way ahead, as his habit was, his shoulders humped, his eyes fixed on the straight gray road in front of him; so he did not notice poor Mole when suddenly the summons reached him, and took him like an electric shock.

We others, who have long lost the more subtle of the physical senses, have not even proper terms to express an animal's intercommunications with his surroundings, living or otherwise, and have only the word "smell," for instance, to include the whole range of delicate thrills which murmur in the nose of the animal night and day, summoning, warning, inciting, repelling.

It was one of these mysterious fairy calls from out the void that suddenly reached Mole in the darkness, making him tingle through and through with its very familiar appeal, even while as yet he could not clearly remember what it was. He stopped dead in his tracks, his nose searching hither and thither in its efforts to recapture the fine filament, the telegraphic current, that had so strongly moved him. A moment, and he had caught it again; and with it this time came recollection in fullest flood.

Home! That was what they meant, those caressing appeals, those soft touches wafted through the air, those invisible little hands pulling and tugging, all one way! Why, it must be quite close by him at that moment, his old home that he had hurriedly forsaken and never sought again, that day when he first found the river!

And now it was sending out its scouts and its messengers to capture him and bring him in. Since his escape on that bright morning he had hardly given it a thought, so absorbed had he been in his new life, in all its pleasures, its surprises, its fresh and captivating experiences. Now, with a rush of old memories, how clearly it stood up before him, in the darkness! Shabby indeed, and small and poorly furnished, and yet his, the home he had made for himself, the home he had been so happy to get back to after his day's work. And the home had been happy with him, too, evidently, and was missing him, and wanted him back, and was telling him so, through his nose, sorrowfully, reproachfully, but with no bitterness or anger; only with plaintive reminder that it was there, and wanted him.

The call was clear, the summons was plain. He must obey it instantly, and go.

"Ratty!" he called, full of joyful excitement. "Hold on! Come back! I want you quick!"

"O, come along, Mole, do!" replied the Rat cheerfully, still plodding along.

"Please stop, Ratty!" pleaded the poor Mole, in anguish of heart. "You don't understand! It's my home, my old home! I've just come across the smell of it, and it's close by here, really quite close. And I must go to it, I must, I must! O, come back, Ratty! Please, please come back!"

The Rat was by this time very far ahead, too far to hear clearly what the Mole was calling, too far to catch the sharp note of painful appeal in his voice. And he was much taken up with the weather, for he too could smell something—something suspiciously like approaching snow.

"Mole, we mustn't stop now, really!" he called back. "We'll come for it tomorrow, whatever it is you've found. But I daren't stop now—it's late, and the snow's coming on again, and I'm not sure of the way! And I want your nose, Mole, so come on quick, there's a good fellow!"

And the Rat pressed forward on his way without waiting for an answer.

Poor Mole stood alone in the road, his heart torn asunder, and a big sob gathering, gathering, somewhere low down inside him, to leap up to the surface presently, he knew, in passionate escape. But even under such a test as this his loyalty to his friend stood firm. Never for a moment did he dream of abandoning him. Meanwhile, the wafts from his old home pleaded, whispered, conjured, and finally claimed him imperiously. He dared not tarry longer within their magic circle. With a wrench that tore his very heartstrings he set his face down the road and followed submissively in the track of the Rat, while faint, thin little smells, still dogging his retreating nose, reproached him for his new friendship and his callous forgetfulness.

With an effort he caught up the unsuspecting Rat, who began chattering cheerfully about what they would do when they got back, and how jolly a fire of logs in the parlor would be, and what a supper he meant to eat; never noticing his companion's silence and distressful state of mind. At last, however, when they had gone some considerable way further, and were passing some tree-stumps at the edge of a copse that bordered the road, he stopped and said kindly, "Look here, Mole, old chap, you seem dead tired. No talk left in you, and your feet dragging like lead. We'll sit down here for a minute and rest. The snow has held off so far, and the best part of our journey is over."

The Mole subsided forlornly on a tree-stump and tried to control himself, for he felt it surely coming. The sob he had fought with so long refused to be beaten. Up and up, it forced its way to the air, and then another, and another, and others thick and fast; till poor Mole at last gave up the struggle, and cried freely and helplessly and openly, now that he knew it was all over and he had lost what he could hardly be said to have found.

The Rat, astonished and dismayed at the violence of Mole's paroxysm of grief, did not dare to speak for a while. At last he said, very quietly and sympathetically, "What is it, old fellow? Whatever can be the matter? Tell us your trouble, and let me see what I can do."

Poor Mole found it difficult to get any words out between the upheavals of his chest that followed one upon another so quickly and held back speech and choked it as it came. "I know it's a—shabby, dingy little place," he sobbed forth at last, brokenly, "not like—your cozy quarters—or Toad's beautiful hall—or Badger's great house—but it was my own little home—and I was fond of it—and I went away and forgot all about it—and then I smelt it suddenly on the road, when I called and you wouldn't listen, Rat—and everything came back to me with a rush—and I wanted it! O dear,

O dear!—and when you wouldn't turn back, Ratty—and I had to leave it, though I was smelling it all the time—I thought my heart would break. We might have just gone and had one look at it, Ratty—only one look—it was close by—but you wouldn't turn back, Ratty, you wouldn't turn back! O dear, O dear!"

Recollection brought fresh waves of sorrow, and sobs again took full charge of him, preventing further speech. The Rat stared straight in front of him, saying nothing, only patting Mole gently on the shoulder. After a time he muttered gloomily, "I see it all now! What a pig I have been! A pig—that's me! Just a pig—a plain pig!"

He waited till Mole's sobs became gradually less stormy and more rhythmical; he waited till at last sniffs were frequent and sobs only intermittent. Then he rose from his seat, and, remarking carelessly, "Well, now we'd really better be getting on, old chap!" set off up the road again, over the toilsome way they had come.

"Wherever are you (hic) going to (hic), Ratty?" cried the tearful Mole, looking up in alarm.

"We're going to find that home of yours, old fellow," replied the Rat pleasantly; "so you had better come along, for it will take some finding, and we shall want your nose."

"O, come back, Ratty, do!" cried the Mole, getting up and hurrying after him. "It's no good, I tell you! It's too late, and too dark, and the place is too far off, and the snow's coming! And—and I never meant to let you know I was feeling that way about it—it was all an accident and a mistake! And think of River Bank, and your supper!"

"Hang River Bank, and supper too!" said the Rat heartily. "I tell you, I'm going to find this place now, if I stay out all night. So cheer up, old chap, and take my arm, and we'll very soon be back there again."

Still snuffling, pleading, and reluctant, Mole suffered himself to be dragged back along the road by his imperious companion, who by a flow of cheerful talk and anecdote endeavored to beguile his spirits back and make the weary way seem shorter. When at last it seemed to the Rat that they must be nearing that part of the road where Mole had been "held up," he said, "Now, no more talking. Business! Use your nose, and give your mind to it."

They moved on in silence for some little way, when suddenly the Rat was conscious, through his arm that was linked in Mole's, of a faint sort of electric thrill that was passing down that animal's body. Instantly he disengaged himself, fell back a pace, and waited, all attention.

The signals were coming through!

Mole stood a moment rigid, while his uplifted nose, quivering slightly, felt the air.

Then a short, quick run forward—a fault—a check—a try back; and then a slow, steady, confident advance.

The Rat, much excited, kept close to his heels as the Mole, with something of the air of a sleepwalker, crossed a dry ditch, scrambled through a hedge, and nosed his way over a field open and trackless and bare in the faint starlight.

Suddenly, without giving warning, he dived; but the Rat was on the alert, and promptly followed him down the tunnel to which his unerring nose had faithfully led him.

It was close and airless, and the earthy smell was strong, and it seemed a long time to Rat before the passage ended and he could stand erect and stretch and shake himself. The Mole struck a match, and by its light the Rat saw that they

were standing in an open space, neatly swept and sanded underfoot, and directly facing them was Mole's little front door, with "Mole End" painted, in Gothic lettering, over the bell-pull at the side.

Mole reached down a lantern from a nail on the wall and lit it, and the Rat, looking round him, saw that they were in a sort of fore-court. A garden-seat stood on one side of the door, and on the other, a roller; for the Mole, who was a tidy animal when at home, could not stand having his ground kicked up by other animals into little runs that ended in earth-heaps. On the walls hung wire baskets with ferns in them, alternating with brackets carrying plaster statuary— Garibaldi, and the infant Samuel, and Queen Victoria, and other heroes of modern Italy. Down one side of the fore-court ran a skittle-alley, with benches along it and little wooden tables marked with rings that hinted at beer-mugs. In the middle was a small round pond containing goldfish and surrounded by a cockle-shell border. Out of the center of the pond rose a fanciful structure clothed in more cockle-shells and topped by a large silvered glass ball that reflected everything all wrong and had a very pleasing effect.

Mole's face beamed at the sight of all these objects so dear to him, and he hurried Rat through the door, lit a lamp in the hall, and took one glance round his old home. He saw the dust lying thick on everything, saw the cheerless, deserted look of the long-neglected house, and its narrow, meager dimensions, its worn and shabby contents—and collapsed again on a hall-chair, his nose in his paws.

"O, Ratty!" he cried dismally. "Why ever did I do it? Why did I bring you to this poor, cold little place, on a night like this, when you might have been at River Bank by this time, toasting your toes before a blazing fire, with all your nice things about you!"

The Rat paid no heed to his doleful self-reproaches. He was running here and there, opening ...doors, inspecting rooms and cupboards, and lighting lamps and candles and sticking them up everywhere. "What a capital little house this is!" he called out cheerily. "So compact! So well planned! Everything here and everything in its place! We'll make a jolly night of it. The first thing we want is a good fire; I'll see to that—I always know where to find things. So this is the parlor? Splendid! Your own idea, those little sleeping-bunks in the wall? Capital! Now, I'll fetch the wood and the coals, and you get a duster, Mole—you'll find one in the drawer of the kitchen table—and try and smarten things up a bit. Bustle about, old chap!"

Encouraged by his inspiriting companion, the Mole roused himself and dusted and polished with energy and heartiness, while the Rat, running to and fro with armfuls of fuel, soon had a cheerful blaze roaring up the chimney. He hailed the Mole to come and warm himself; but Mole promptly had another fit of the blues, dropping down on a couch in dark despair and burying his face in his duster.

"Rat," he moaned, "how about your supper, you poor, cold, hungry, weary animal? I've nothing to give you— nothing—not a crumb!"

"What a fellow you are for giving in!" said the Rat reproachfully. "Why, only just now I saw a sardine-opener on the kitchen dresser, quite distinctly; and everybody knows that means there are sardines about somewhere in the neighborhood. Rouse yourself! Pull yourself together, and come with me and forage."

They went and foraged accordingly, hunting through every cupboard and turning out every drawer.

The result was not so very depressing after all, though of course it might have been better; a tin of sardines—a box of captain's biscuits, nearly full—and a German sausage encased in silver paper.

"There's a banquet for you!" observed the Rat, as he arranged the table. "I know some animals who would give their ears to be sitting down to supper with us tonight!"

"No bread!" groaned the Mole; "no butter, no—"

"No pâté de foie gras, no champagne!" continued the Rat, grinning. "And that reminds me—what's that little door at the end of the passage? Your cellar, of course! Every luxury in this house! Just you wait a minute."

He made for the cellar door, and presently reappeared, somewhat dusty, with a bottle of beer in each paw and another under each arm.

"Self-indulgent beggar you seem to be, Mole," he observed. "Deny yourself nothing. This is really the jolliest little place I ever was in. Now, wherever did you pick up those prints? Make the place look so home-like, they do. No wonder you're so fond of it, Mole. Tell us about it, and how you came to make it what it is."

Then, while the Rat busied himself fetching plates, and knives and forks, and mustard which he mixed in an egg-cup, the Mole, his bosom still heaving with the stress of his recent emotion, related—somewhat shyly at first, but with more freedom as he warmed to his subject—how this was planned, and how that was thought out, and how this was got through a windfall from an aunt, and that was a wonderful find and a bargain, and this other thing was bought out of laborious savings and a certain amount of "going without." His spirits finally quite restored, he had to go and caress his possessions, and show off their points to his visitor and expatiate on them, quite forgetful of the supper they both so much needed; Rat, who was desperately hungry but strove to conceal it, nodding seriously, examining with a puckered brow, and saying, "Wonderful," and "Most remarkable," at intervals, when the chance for an observation was given him.

At last the Rat succeeded in decoying him to the table, and had just got seriously to work with the sardine-opener when sounds were heard from the fore-court without— sounds like the scuffling of small feet in the gravel and a confused murmur of tiny voices, while broken sentences reached them—"Now, all in a line—hold the lantern up a bit, Tommy—clear your throats first—no coughing after I say one, two, three. Where's young Bill?—Here, come on, do, we're all a-waiting—"

"What's up?" inquired the Rat, pausing in his labors.

"I think it must be the field-mice," replied the Mole, with a touch of pride in his manner. "They go round carol-singing regularly at this time of the year. They're quite an institution in these parts. And they never pass me over—they come to Mole End last of all; and I used to give them hot drinks, and supper too sometimes, when I could afford it. It will be like old times to hear them again."

"Let's have a look at them!" cried the Rat, jumping up and running to the door.

It was a pretty sight, and a seasonable one, that met their eyes when they flung the door open. In the fore-court, lit by the dim rays of a horn lantern, some eight or ten little field-mice stood in a semi-circle, red worsted comforters round their throats, their fore-paws thrust deep into their pockets, their feet jigging for warmth. With bright beady eyes they glanced shyly at each other, sniggering a little, sniffing and applying coat-sleeves a good deal. As the door opened, one of the elder ones that carried the lantern was just saying, "Now then, one, two, three!" and forthwith their shrill little voices uprose on the air, singing one of the old-time carols that their forefathers composed in fields that were fallow and held by frost, or when snow-bound in chimney corners, and handed down to be sung in the miry street to lamp-lit windows at Yule-time.

CAROL

Villagers all, this frosty tide,
Let your doors swing open wide,
Though wind may follow, and snow beside,
Yet draw us in by your fire to bide;
    Joy shall be yours in the morning!

Here we stand in the cold and the sleet,
Blowing fingers and stamping feet,
Come from far away you to greet—
You by the fire and we in the street—
    Bidding you joy in the morning!

Fore ere one half of the night was gone,
Sudden a star has led us on,
Raining bliss and benison—
Bliss tomorrow and more anon,
    Joy for every morning!

Goodman Joseph toiled through the snow—
Saw the star o'er a stable low;
Mary she might not further go—
Welcome thatch, and litter below!
    Joy was hers in the morning!

And then they heard the angels tell
"Who were the first to cry Nowell?
Animals all, as it befell,
In the stable where they did dwell!
    Joy shall be theirs in the morning!"

The voices ceased, the singers, bashful but smiling, exchanged sidelong glances, and silence succeeded—but for a moment only. Then, from up above and far away, down the tunnel they had so lately traveled was borne to their ears in a faint musical hum the sound of distant bells ringing a joyful and clangorous peal.

"Very well sung, boys!" cried the Rat heartily. "And now come along in, all of you, and warm yourselves by the fire, and have something hot!"

"Yes, come along, field-mice," cried the Mole eagerly. "This is quite like old times! Shut the door after you. Pull up that settle to the fire. Now, you just wait a minute, while we—O, Ratty!" he cried in despair, plumping down on a seat, with tears impending. "Whatever are we doing? We've nothing to give them!"

"You leave all that to me," said the masterful Rat. "Here, you with the lantern! Come over this way. I want to talk to you. Now, tell me, are there any shops open at this hour of the night?"

"Why, certainly, sir," replied the field-mouse respectfully. "At this time of the year our shops keep open to all hours."

"Then look here!" said the Rat. "You go off at once, you and your lantern, and you get me—"

Here much muttered conversation ensued, and the Mole only heard bits of it, such as—"Fresh, mind!—no, a pound of that will do—see you get Buggins's, for I won't have any other—no, only the best—if you can't get it there, try somewhere else—yes, of course, home-made, no tinned stuff—well then, do the best you can!" Finally, there was a chink of coin passing from paw to paw, the field-mouse was provided with an ample basket for his purchases, and off he hurried, he and his lantern.

The rest of the field-mice, perched in a row on the settle, their small legs swinging, gave themselves up to enjoyment of the fire, and toasted their chilblains till they tingled; while the Mole, failing to draw them into easy conversation, plunged into family history and made each of them recite the names of his numerous brothers, who were too young, it appeared, to be allowed to go out a-caroling this year, but looked forward very shortly to winning the parental consent.

The Rat, meanwhile, was busy examining the label on one of the beer-bottles. "I perceive this to be Old Burton," he remarked approvingly. "Sensible Mole! The very thing! Now we shall be able to mull some ale! Get the things ready, Mole, while I draw the corks."

It did not take long to prepare the brew and thrust the tin heater well into the red heart of the fire; and soon every field-mouse was sipping and coughing and choking (for a little mulled ale goes a long way) and wiping his eyes and laughing and forgetting he had ever been cold in all his life.

"They act plays too, these fellows," the Mole explained to the rat. "Make them up all by themselves, and act them afterward. And very well they do it, too! They gave us a capital one last year, about a field-mouse who was captured at sea by a Barbary corsair, and made to row in a galley; and when he escaped and got home again, his lady-love had gone into a convent. Here, you! You were in it, I remember. Get up and recite a bit."

The field-mouse addressed got up on his legs, giggled shyly, looked round the room, and remained absolutely tongue-tied. His comrades cheered him on, Mole coaxed and encouraged him, and the Rat went so far as to take him by the shoulders and shake him; but nothing could overcome his stage-fright.

They were all busily engaged on him like water men applying the Royal Humane Society's regulations to a case of long submersion, when the latch clicked, the door opened, and the field-mouse with the lantern reappeared, staggering under the weight of his basket.

There was no more talk of play-acting once the real and solid contents of the basket had been tumbled out on the table. Under the generalship of Rat, everybody was set to do something. In a few minutes supper was ready, and Mole, as he took the head of the table in a sort of dream, saw a lately barren board set thick with savory comforts; saw his little friends' faces brighten and beam as they fell to without delay; and then let himself loose—for he was famished indeed—on the provender so magically provided, thinking what a happy homecoming this had turned out, after all.

As they ate, they talked of old times, and the field-mice gave him the local gossip up to date, and answered as well as they could the hundred questions he had to ask them. The Rat said little or nothing, only taking care that each guest had what he wanted, and plenty of it, and that Mole had no trouble or anxiety about anything.

They clattered off at last, very grateful and showering wishes of the season, with their jacket pockets stuffed with remembrances for the small brothers and sisters at home. When the door had closed on the last of them and the chink of the lanterns had died away, Mole and Rat kicked the fire up, drew their chairs in, brewed themselves a last nightcap of mulled ale, and discussed the events of the long day. At last the Rat, with a tremendous yawn, said, "Mole, old chap, I'm ready to drop. Sleepy is simply not the word. That your own bunk over on that side? Very well, then, I'll take this. What a ripping little house this is! Everything so handy!"

He clambered into his bunk and rolled himself well up in the blankets, and slumber gathered him forthwith, as a swath of barley is folded into the arms of the reaping-machine.

The weary Mole also was glad to turn in without delay, and soon had his head on his pillow, in great joy and contentment. But before he closed his eyes he let them wander round his old room, mellow in the glow of the firelight that played or rested on familiar and friendly things which had long been unconsciously a part of him, and now smilingly received him back, without rancor.

He was now in just the frame of mind that the tactful Rat had quietly worked to bring about in him. He saw clearly how plain and simple—how narrow, even—it all was; but clearly, too, how much it all meant to him, and the special value of some such anchorage in one's existence. He did not at all want to abandon the new life and its splendid spaces, to turn his back on sun and air and all they offered him and creep home and stay there; the upper world was all too strong, it called to him still, even down there, and he knew he must return to the larger stage.

But it was good to think he had this to come back to, this place which was all his own, these things which were so glad to see him again and could always be counted upon for the same simple welcome.

MINSTRELS

by William Wordsworth

Considering his tumultuous background, the success of poet William Wordsworth is extraordinary. Born on April 7, 1770, in Cumberland, England, Wordsworth lost his mother to illness when he was only eight. Then, just five years later, his father died, leaving Wordsworth and his three brothers to board with a woman named Ann Tyson while they attended Hawkshead Grammar School near Esthwaite Lake. It was during this time when Wordsworth wrote his first lines of verse about summer vacation.

Then, in 1787, when he was just seventeen, he published his first poem, "Sonnet, On Seeing Miss Helen Maria Williams Weep at a Tale of Distress" in European Magazine.

In the fall of that year, young Wordsworth attended St. John's Cambridge, but left in the middle of his studies to do what his family called "mad and dangerous." He traveled to Europe with a friend to take a walking tour of the Alps. This trip was especially daring because France was in the middle of a revolution. Luckily, the adventurous poet returned home unscathed, and completed his degree in January 1791.

Wordsworth did, however, return to France a year later, where he met and fell in love with a woman named Annette Vallon. In 1792, the couple had a baby, but unfortunately by this time, Wordsworth found himself too short of funds to remain in France and had to return to England alone.

Back in England, Wordsworth was very depressed. But then, just when he was at his lowest, a friend died, leaving him a good deal of money, allowing him to settle down with his sister, Dorothy, in a cottage at Racedown, Dorsetshire. It was at this time that Wordsworth met the famous poet, Samuel Taylor Coleridge, with whom he composed a great deal of poetry. Also produced from this friendship was a small, brilliant volume of work entitled, Lyrical Ballads, with a Few Other Poems, which was published in 1798.

After receiving a much-delayed inheritance from his father, Wordsworth married Mary Hutchinson, a Lake Country woman whom he had known since childhood. Although it was about this time that his prosperity and reputation greatly improved, he also went through many personal hardships. His brother John drowned in 1805, two of his five children died in 1812, and Dorothy's health began to decline. In addition to this family tragedy, Wordsworth also got into a quarrel with Coleridge, which lasted twenty years.

Among other notable achievements, Wordsworth received several honorary degrees from reputed universities and was appointed poet laureate in 1843. But due to his love of the great outdoors, and his fondness for walking in all types of weather, Wordsworth came down with pleurisy in 1850. Soon after, on April 23 of that year, he died at the age of eighty, leaving behind a huge collection of prodigious works that readers and scholars find fascinating to this day.

Wordsworth's lilting prose appears in the poem "Minstrels,"
where a group of players, guided by the inspiring scenery of the
Yuletide season, bring Christmas tidings to those all around them.

The minstrels played their Christmas tune
  Tonight beneath my cottage-eaves;
While, smitten by a lofty moon,
  The encircling laurels, thick with leaves,
Gave back a rich and dazzling sheen,
That overpowered their natural green.

Through hill and valley every breeze
  Had sunk to rest with folded wings:
Keen was the air, but could not freeze,
  Nor check, the music of the strings;
So stout and hardy were the band
That scraped the chords with strenuous hand.

And who but listened?—till was paid
  Respect to every inmate's claim,
The greeting given, the music played
  In honor of each household name,
Duly pronounced with lusty call,
And "Merry Christmas" wished to all.

Dashing through the snow,
  In a one-horse open sleigh:
O'er the fields we go,
  Laughing all the way.

Words and music by J. S. Pierpont
from his song, "Jingle Bells" [1857]

THE MOUSE THAT DIDN'T BELIEVE IN SANTA CLAUS

by Eugene Field

Born and raised in St. Louis, Missouri, the popular humorist and newspaperman, Eugene Field, claimed two dates for his birthday—September 2 and 3, 1850—so if his friends forgot the first day, they could remember the second. Raised by his cousin in Amherst, Massachusetts after his mother's death in 1856, Field did remain in contact with his father, Roswell M. Reed, a lawyer who gained fame for successfully defending a fugitive slave named Dred Scott.

Field began college at Williams in 1868, but left when his father died the following spring. He then enrolled in Knox College at Galesburg, Illinois, and then transferred again to the University of Missouri at Columbia the next year. Although he was known for his wit, Field was never a serious student and dropped out of college before graduation, and in 1871, he received an inheritance from his father's estate, and spent some time traveling in Europe. Two years later, he married Julia Sutherland Comstock, and the couple had eight children.

For the next eight years, Field worked on several newspapers in Missouri—the St. Louis Evening Journal, St. Joseph Gazette, St. Louis Times-Journal, and the Kansas City Times—and in 1881 he moved to Denver where he wrote for the Denver Tribune. Two years later the family moved to Chicago and Field wrote a column called "Sharps and Flats" for the Chicago Morning News for the next twelve years.

By the time he moved to Chicago, Field had a large following of readers. He had already published a book in 1881 called The Tribune Primer, a collection of articles from the Denver Tribune. But what really won Field long-lasting fame was the poem "Little Boy Blue," also published that year in a weekly journal called America. After this success, Field wrote poetry prolifically. In 1889 he published A Little Book of Western Verse followed by A Second Book of Verse and With Trumpet and Drum, both published in 1892, and Love-Songs of Childhood in 1894. These books established him as the "poet of children," and with his death of heart failure in 1895, several schools in American cities were named after him, and the state of Missouri held "Eugene Field Days" to commemorate the anniversary date of his death.

Although he was mostly known for his poetry, Field also wrote some short stories. In "The Mouse that Didn't Believe in Santa Claus," a silly young mouse named Squeaknibble disobeys her mother on Christmas Eve when she stays up late after being told to go to sleep and wait for Santa Claus to bring her some lovely bits of cheese. But Squeaknibble learns her lesson when she comes face to face with the legendary gift-giver—only to find that he has gleaming white fangs and razor-sharp claws!

The clock stood, of course, in the corner, a moonbeam floated idly on the floor, and a little mauve mouse came from the hole in the chimney corner and frisked and scampered in the light of the moonbeam upon the floor. The little mauve mouse was particularly merry; sometimes she danced upon two legs and sometimes upon four legs, but always very daintily and always very merrily.

"Ah, me!" sighed the old clock, "how different mice are nowadays from the mice we used to have in the good old times! Now there was your grandma, Mistress Velvetpaw, and there was your grandpa, Master Sniffwhisker—how grave and dignified they were! Many a night have I seen them dancing upon the carpet below me, but always the stately minuet and never that crazy frisking which you are executing now, to my surprise—yes, and to my horror, too."

"But why shouldn't I be merry?" asked the little mauve mouse. "Tomorrow is Christmas, and this is Christmas Eve."

"So it is," said the old clock. "I had really forgotten all about it. But, tell me, what is Christmas to you, little Miss Mauve Mouse?"

"A great deal to me!" cried the little mauve mouse. "I have been very good a very long time: I have not used any bad words, nor have I gnawed any holes, nor have I stolen any canary seed, nor have I worried my mother by running behind the flour-barrel where that horrid trap is set. In fact, I have been so good that I'm very sure Santa Claus will bring me something very pretty."

This seemed to amuse the old clock mightily; in fact, the old clock fell to laughing so heartily that in an unguarded moment she struck twelve instead of ten, which was exceedingly careless and therefore to be reprehended.

"Why, you silly little mauve mouse," said the old clock, "you don't believe in Santa Claus, do you?"

"Of course I do," answered the little mauve mouse. "Why shouldn't I? Didn't Santa Claus bring me a beautiful butter-cracker last Christmas, and a lovely gingersnap, and a delicious rind of cheese? I should be very ungrateful if I did not believe in Santa Claus, and I certainly shall not disbelieve in him at the very moment when I am expecting him to arrive with a bundle of goodies for me.

"I once had a little sister," continued the little mauve mouse, "who did not believe in Santa Claus, and the very thought of the fate that befell her makes my blood run cold and my whiskers stand on end. She died before I was born, but my mother told me all about her. Perhaps you never saw her; her name was Squeaknibble, and she was in stature one of those long, low, rangy mice that are seldom found in well-stocked pantries. Mother says that Squeaknibble took after our ancestors who came from New England, where the malignant ingenuity of the people and the ferocity of the cats rendered life precarious indeed.

"Squeaknibble seemed to inherit many ancestral traits, the most conspicuous of which was a disposition to sneer at some of the most respected dogmas in mousedom. From her very infancy she doubted, for example, the widely accepted theory that the moon was composed of green cheese; and this heresy was the first intimation her parents had of the skeptical turn of her mind. Of course, her parents were vastly annoyed, for their maturer natures saw that this youthful skepticism portended serious, if not fatal, consequences. Yet all in vain did the sagacious couple reason and plead with their headstrong and heretical child.

"For a long time Squeaknibble would not believe that there was any such archfiend as a cat; but she came to be convinced to the contrary one memorable night, on which occasion she lost two inches of her beautiful tail, and received so terrible a fright that for fully an hour afterward her little heart beat so violently as to lift her off her feet and bump her head against the top of our domestic hole. The cat, the same brindled ogress, nowadays steals into this room, crouches treacherously behind the sofa, and feigns to be asleep, hoping, forsooth, that some of us, heedless of her hated presence, will venture within reach of her diabolical claws. So enraged was this ferocious monster at the escape of my sister that she ground her fangs viciously together, and vowed to take no pleasure in life until she held in her devouring jaws the innocent little mouse which belonged to the mangled bit of tail she even then clutched in her remorseless claws."

"Yes," said the old clock, "now that you recall the incident, I recollect it well. I was here then, in this very corner, and I remember that I laughed at the cat and chided her for her awkwardness. My reproaches irritated her; she told me that a clock's duty was to run itself down not to be depreciating the merits of others! Yes, I recall the time; that cat's tongue is fully as sharp as her claws."

"Be that as it may," said the little mauve mouse, "it is a matter of history, and therefore beyond dispute, that from that very moment the cat pined for Squeaknibble's life; it seemed as if that one little two-inch taste of Squeaknibble's tail had filled the cat with a consuming passion, or appetite, for the rest of Squeaknibble. So the cat waited and watched and hunted and schemed and devised and did everything possible for a cat—a cruel cat—to do in order to gain her

murderous ends. One night—one fatal Christmas Eve—our mother had undressed the children for bed, and was urging upon them to go to sleep earlier than usual, since she fully expected that Santa Claus would bring each of them something very palatable and nice before morning. Thereupon the little dears whisked their cunning tails, pricked up their beautiful ears, and began telling one another what they hoped Santa Claus would bring. One asked for a slice of Roquefort, another for Neufchatel, another for Sap Sago, and a fourth Edam; one expressed a preference for de Brie, while another hoped to get Parmesan; one clamored for imperial blue Stilton, and another craved the fragrant boon of Caprera. There were fourteen little ones then, and consequently diverse opinions as to the kind of gift Santa Claus should best bring; still, there was, as you can readily understand, an enthusiastic unanimity upon this point, namely, that the gift should be cheese of some brand or other.

"'My dears,' said our mother, 'what matters is whether the boon which Santa Claus brings be royal English cheddar or fromage de Bricquebec, Vermont sage, or Herkimer County skim-milk? We should be content with whatsoever Santa Claus bestows, so long as it be cheese, disjoined from all traps whatsoever, unmixed with Paris green, and free from glass, strychnine, and other harmful ingredients. As for myself, I shall be satisfied with a cut of nice, fresh Western reserve; for truly I recognize in no other viand or edible half the fragrance or half the gustfulness to be met with in one of these pale but aromatic domestic products. So run away to your dreams now, that Santa Claus may find you sleeping.'

"The children obeyed—all but Squeaknibble. 'Let the others think what they please,' said she, 'but I don't believe in Santa Claus. I'm not going to bed, either. I'm going to creep out of this dark hole and have a quiet romp, all by myself, in the moonlight.' Oh, what a vain, foolish, wicked little mouse was Squeaknibble! But I will not reproach the dead; her punishment came all too swiftly. Now listen: who do you suppose overheard her talking so disrespectfully of Santa Claus?"

"Why, Santa Claus himself," said the old clock.

"Oh, no," answered the little mauve mouse. "It was that wicked, murderous cat! It lies in wait for naughty little mice. And you can depend upon it that, when that awful cat heard Squeaknibble speak so disrespectfully of Santa Claus, her wicked eyes glowed with joy, her sharp teeth watered, and her bristling fur emitted electric sparks as big as marrowfat peas. Then what did that blood-thirsty monster do but scuttle as fast as she could into Dear-my-Soul's room, leap up into Dear-my-Soul's crib, and walk off with the pretty little white muff which Dear-my-Soul used to wear when she went for a visit to the little girl in the next block! What upon earth did the horrid old cat want with Dear-my-Soul's pretty little white muff? Ah, the duplicity, the diabolical ingenuity of that!

"In the first place," resumed the little mauve mouse, after a pause that testified to the depth of her emotion—"that wretched cat dressed herself up in that pretty little white muff, by which you are to understand that she crawled through the muff just so far as to leave her four cruel legs at liberty."

"Yes, I understand," said the old clock.

"Then she put on the boy doll's fur cap," said the little mauve mouse, "and when she was arrayed in the boy doll's fur cap and Dear-my-Soul's little white muff, of course she didn't look like a cruel cat at all. But whom did she look like?"

"Like the boy doll," suggested the old clock.

"No, no!" cried the little mauve mouse.

"Like Dear-my-Soul?" asked the old clock.

"How stupid you are!" exclaimed the little mauve mouse. "Why, she looked like Santa Claus, of course!"

"Oh, yes; I see," said the old clock. "Now I begin to be interested; go on."

"Alas!" sighed the little mauve mouse, "not much remains to be told; but there is more of my story left than there was of Squeaknibble when that horrid cat crawled out of that miserable disguise. You are to understand that, contrary to her sagacious mother's injunction, and in notorious derision of the mooted coming of Santa Claus, Squeaknibble issued from the friendly hole in the chimney corner, and gamboled about over this very carpet, and, I dare say, in this very moonlight.

"Right merrily was Squeaknibble gamboling," continued the little mauve mouse, "and she had just turned a double back somersault without the use of what remained of her tail, when, all of a sudden, she beheld, looming up like a monster ghost, a figure all in white fur! Oh, how frightened she was, and how her little heart did beat! 'Purr, purr-r-r,' said the ghost in white fur. 'Oh, please don't hurt me!' pleaded Squeaknibble. 'No; I'll not hurt you,' said the ghost in white fur; 'I'm Santa Claus, and I've brought you a beautiful piece of savory old cheese, you dear little mousie, you.' Poor Squeaknibble was deceived; a skeptic all her life, she was at last befooled by the most palpable and most fatal of frauds. 'How good of you!' said Squeaknibble. 'I didn't believe there was a Santa Claus, and—' but before she could say more she was seized by two sharp, cruel claws that conveyed her crushed body to the murderous mouth of mousedom's most malignant foe. I can dwell no longer upon this harrowing scene. Suffice it to say that before the morrow's sun rose like a big yellow Herkimer County cheese upon the spot where that tragedy had been enacted, poor Squeaknibble passed to that bourn whence two inches of her beautiful tail had preceded her by the space of three weeks to a day. As for Santa Claus, when he came that Christmas eve, bringing *morceaux de Brie* and of Stilton for the other little mice, he heard with sorrow of Squeaknibble's fate; and before he departed he said that in all his experience he had never known of a mouse or of a child that had prospered after once saying that he didn't believe in Santa Claus."

New Relations and Duties

by Frederick Douglass

Because he was born a slave, Frederick Douglass—born Frederick Augustus Washington Bailey—was never sure of his exact date of birth, but he calculated it to be in February of 1817. His mother, Harriet Bailey, was a literate slave, but he saw very little of her, and was raised by his grandparents for the first few years of his life.

In 1826 Douglass was sent to Baltimore, Maryland to take care of a family. The mistress of the house, Sophia Auld, took a liking to Douglass and began teaching him how to read. But when her husband Hugh found out, he forbade her to continue, so Douglass found ways to teach himself to read and write. On September 3, 1838, Douglass escaped with the help of freedwoman Anna Murray. He then boarded a train disguised as a sailor and made it to New York. Once there, Murray came from Baltimore, and the two were married twelve days later. It was at this time that he changed his name to Douglass after a character in Sir Walter Scott's Lady of the Lake.

After working at various jobs for a few years, Douglass attended an antislavery convention in Nantucket in 1841. While there, he was asked to say a few words about his experience as a slave. His speech was so moving that he was asked to become a fugitive slave lecturer, a position which lasted for four years. In 1845 he wrote down the stories that he had been telling as a lecturer in the Narrative of the Life of Frederick Douglass, an American Slave. Once this was published, Douglass feared being recaptured, so he fled to England, where he continued to lecture, as well as in Ireland, Scotland, and Wales.

Douglass' friends in England wrote to an attorney and discovered that Captain Thomas Auld, Douglass' original owner, would take $750 to free him. And so finally, on December 5, 1846, his release papers were signed, and he returned to America.

That following year, Douglass began an antislavery paper which was eventually called Frederick Douglass' Paper, and in June 1858 he started Douglass' Monthly, an abolitionist magazine. During this time he had worked closely with Harriet Beecher Stowe, the author of Uncle Tom's Cabin, and reworked and republished his autobiography, calling it My Bondage and My Freedom.

Over the next several years, Douglass' already amazing life took even more remarkable turns. On October 16, 1859, a man named John Brown and eighteen followers attacked the arsenal at Harper's Ferry. As a strong supporter of Brown, Douglass, along with many others, was called to be prosecuted. Although Douglass opposed the actual raid, he still fled to England, fearing for his life. But after hearing of his daughter Annie's death in 1860, Douglass returned to America, where he learned that Brown had been turned into a virtual martyr, implicating no one, and that the whole ordeal was overshadowed by the great debates between Abraham Lincoln and Stephen A. Douglas. At this time, Douglass focused his efforts on allowing blacks in the military, and in time Governor

Andrew of Massachusetts was able to raise two black regiments, of which Douglass' two sons were members.

After the Civil War, Douglass attended the 1866 National Loyalist's Convention as the representative of Rochester, New York. His attendance impressed Ulysses S. Grant, and the 14th and 15th amendments to the Constitution were soon implemented, giving blacks the right to vote. This truly began Douglass' political career, and he was then appointed Council of District of Columbia by President Grant, the United States Marshall of the District of Columbia by President Rutherford B. Hayes, and the Recorder of Deeds for the District of Columbia by President James Garfield. This last position's salary was second only to the president's at this time, and enabled Douglass to buy the house of his dreams. Unfortunately, however, he and Anna only lived there for a year before Anna died on August 4, 1882.

Still holding the position as Recorder of Deeds, but now under President Grover Cleveland, Douglass married his white secretary in 1884. Although this interracial marriage caused controversy in many places, President Cleveland always treated Douglass and his wife as equals. Later, Douglass spoke on the Republican platform on behalf of Benjamin Harrison, who, after winning the election, appointed Douglass to the office of Minister Resident and Counsul-General to the Republic of Haiti and Chargé d'affaires to Santo Domingo in 1889. After a long, full life, Douglass died in 1895, at—approximately—the age of seventy-eight.

In "New Relations and Duties," Douglass gives us a unique view of Christmas in Slavery. Though still not physically free, it is clear that the man's soul and spirit are not in bondage.

Long before daylight I was called up to go to feed, rub, and curry the horses. I obeyed the call, as I should have done had it been made at an earlier hour, for I had brought my mind to a firm resolve during the Sunday's reflection to obey every order, however unreasonable, if it were possible, and if Mr. Covey should then undertake to beat me to defend and protect myself to the best of my ability.

When I was obeying Covey's order, he sneaked into the stable, in his peculiar way, and seizing me suddenly by the leg, he brought me to the stable floor, giving my newly mended body a terrible jar. I now forgot all about my roots, and remembered my pledge to stand up in my own defense.

Whence came the daring spirit necessary to grapple with a man who, eight-and-forty hours before, could, with his slightest word, have made me tremble like a leaf in a storm, I do not know; at any rate, *I was resolved to fight*, and what was better still, I actually was hard at it. Every blow of his was parried, though I dealt no blows in return. I was strictly on the *defensive*, preventing him from injuring me, rather than trying to injure him.

All was fair thus far, and the contest was about equal. My resistance was entirely unexpected and Covey was taken aback by it. He trembled in every limb.

"*Are you going to resist*, you scoundrel?" said he.

To which I returned a polite, "Yes, sir."

Taken completely by surprise, Covey seemed to have lost his usual strength and coolness. He was frightened, and stood puffing and blowing, seemingly unable to command words or blows.

At length (two hours had elapsed) the contest was given over. Letting go of me, puffing and blowing at a great rate,

Covey said: "Now, you scoundrel, go to your work: I would not have whipped you half so hard if you had not resisted."

The fact was, he had not whipped me at all.

During the whole six months that I lived with Covey after this transaction, he never again laid the weight of his finger on me in anger. He would occasionally say he did not want to have to get hold of me again—a declaration which I had no difficulty believing.

This battle with Mr. Covey was the turning point in my "life as a slave." It rekindled in my breast the smoldering embers of liberty. It brought up my Baltimore dreams and revived a sense of my own manhood. I was a changed being after that fight. I was *nothing* before; *I was a man* now, with renewed determination to be a free man. I had reached the point at which *I was not afraid to die.* This spirit made me a free man in fact, though I still remained a slave.

My term of service with Edward Covey expired on Christmas day, 1834. I gladly-enough left him, although he was by this time as gentle as a lamb. My home for the year 1835 was already secured, my next master selected. There was always more or less excitement about the changing hands, but determined to fight my way, I had become somewhat reckless and cared little into whose hands I fell. The report got abroad that I was hard to whip; that I was guilty of kicking back, and that, though generally a good-natured Negro, I sometimes "got the devil in me." These sayings were rife in Talbot County and distinguished me among my servile brethren.

Slaves would sometimes fight with each other, and even die at each other's hands, but there were very few who were not held in awe by a white man.

Trained from the cradle up to think and feel that their masters were superiors, and invested with a sort of sacredness, there were few who could rise above the control which that sentiment exercised. I had freed myself from it, and the thing was known. One bad sheep will spoil a whole flock. I was a bad sheep. I hated slavery, slaveholders, and all pertaining to them; and I did not fail to inspire others with the same feeling wherever and whenever opportunity was presented. This made me a marked lad among the slaves, and a suspected one among slaveholders. A knowledge also of my ability to read and write got pretty widely spread, which was very much against me.

The days between Christmas day and New Year's were allowed the slaves as holidays. During these days all regular work was suspended, and there was nothing to do but keep fires and look after the stock. We regarded this time as our own by the grace of our masters, and we therefore used it or abused it as we pleased. Those who had families at a distance were expected to visit them and spend with them the entire week. The younger slaves or the unmarried ones were expected to see to the animals and attend to incidental duties at home.

The holidays were variously spent. The sober, thinking, industrious ones would employ themselves in manufacturing corn-brooms, mats, horse-collars, and baskets, and some of these were very well made. Another class spent their time in hunting opossums, coons, rabbits, and other game. But the majority spent the holidays in sports, ball-playing, wrestling,

boxing, running, foot-races, dancing, and drinking whiskey; and this latter mode was generally most agreeable to their masters. A slave who would work during the holidays was thought by his master undeserving of holidays. There was in this simple act of continued work an accusation against slaves, and a slave could not help thinking that if he made three dollars during the holidays he might make three hundred during the year. Not to be drunk during the holidays was disgraceful.

The fiddling, dancing, and "jubilee beating" was carried on in all directions. This latter performance was strictly southern. It supplied the place of violin or other musical instruments and was played so easily that almost every farm had its "Juba" beater. The performer improvised as he beat the instrument, marking the words as he sang so as to have them fall pat with the movement of his hands. Once in a while among a mass of nonsense and wild frolic, a sharp hit was given to the meanness of slaveholders.

Take the following for example:

We raise de wheat,
Dey gib us de corn;
We bake de bread,
Dey gib us de crust;
We sif de meal,
Dey gib us de huss;

We peel de meat,
Dey gib us de skin;
And dat's de way
Dey take us in.

This is not a bad summary of the palpable injustice and fraud of slavery, as it does, to the lazy and idle the comforts which God designed should be given solely to the honest laborer. But to the holidays. Judging from my own observation and experience, I believe those holidays were among the most effective means in the hands of the slaveholders of keeping down the spirit of insurrection among the slaves.

Joy to the world! the Lord is come;
Let earth receive her King.
Let ev'ry heart prepare Him room,
And heav'n and nature sing.

—Psalm 98 [1719]

Untitled Poem

by Christina Rossetti

Born in *1830*, Christina Rossetti was the sister of the famous painter and poet, Dante Gabriel Rossetti. Helped by her brother to launch her own successful career as a poet, Rossetti lived in England her entire life, though she was greatly influenced by her Italian father. Exiled from Italy, he filled the Rossetti household with politics and culture, and encouraged her and her siblings to develop a love for art and literature.

When she was younger, Rossetti was especially close to her grandfather, Gaetano Polidori, whom she visited often in his country home in Buckinghamshire. By the time she published her first book called Verses in *1847*, Polidori was living in London, and printed it on his own press.

The next year, Rossetti became engaged to a young painter named James Collinson. But being very religious, she would only accept his proposal when he joined the Church of England. Two years later, he converted back to Roman Catholicism and Rossetti broke off the engagement. From this time, Rossetti began publishing poems in several periodicals, including the Athenaeum and the

Germ. *She continued this way until her brother Dante Gabriel beg010 to actively promote her work. In 1861 three of Rossetti's poems appeared in* MacMillan's Magazine, *and the following year* Goblin Market and Other Poems *was brought out by the same publisher.*

Rossetti's health had been poor since adolescence, and in 1871 she contracted Graves' disease. She recovered, but the disease left its mark, not only affecting her heart, but physically disfiguring her eyes with severe swelling. In May 1892 Rossetti underwent surgery for cancer, but the disease was not to be stopped and she died two years later at the age of sixty-four.

In the following untitled poem, Rossetti expresses her strong religious devotion when she thinks of the birth of Christ. She realizes that although others are able to give him material objects, she is able to give him something more meaningful—her heart.

But only His mother
In her maiden bliss
Worshipped the Beloved
   With a kiss.

What can I give Him,
   Poor as I am?
If I were a shepherd
   I would bring a lamb,
If I were a Wise Man
   I would do my part—
Yet what I can I give Him,
   Give my heart.

Silent Night, Holy Night!
All is calm, All is bright . . .

Translated from the German song, "Stille Nacht, Heilige Nacht!" written in 1818 by Joseph Mohr, with music by Franz Gruber.

THE HOLY NIGHT

by Selma Lagerlöf

Novelist Selma Ottiliana Lovisa Lagerlöf was born on November 20, 1858, in the province of Värmland in southern Sweden. At the age of three, she contracted infantile paralysis, and was unable to walk for an entire year. This condition left her with a limp for her entire life, but it certainly didn't slow down her imagination or hamper her success as an author.

Tutored by her grandmother at home throughout her childhood, Lagerlöf attended the Royal Women's Superior Training Academy in Stockholm to prepare for a teaching career in her early twenties. After graduating in 1882, her father died, and the family estate was sold off to pay his debts. Although this came as a severe blow, Lagerlöf quickly accepted a teaching position at a girls' school in southern Sweden and began writing a novel. She entered the first few chapters into a contest given by the Swedish magazine Idun, and not only won, but received an offer from the editor to publish the novel in its entirety. The Story of Gösta Berling *did get published in 1891, but did not become popular until it was praised by the prominent Danish critic, Georg Brandes.*

After the publication of her second book, Invisible Links, *in 1894, Lagerlöf was granted a fellowship by King Oscar and financial assistance from the Swedish Academy. Now able to write full-time, Lagerlöf traveled widely to gather material for subsequent novels. These were so successful that she was able to buy back her family home in 1904, the year in which she won the Gold Medal of the Swedish Academy. Then, in 1909, Lagerlöf became the first woman to win the Nobel Prize in Literature. Inspired by her success, Lagerlöf continued to write, and by the 1920s she was firmly established as one of Sweden's leading writers.*

Not only a talented writer, Lagerlöf was a philanthropist as well, devoting her time to several women's causes, including women's suffrage. During World War II, Lagerlöf helped several German artists and intellectuals escape Nazi persecution, and she donated her gold Nobel Prize medal to a Swedish national fund to benefit Finland, who was under Soviet invasion.

In "The Holy Night," the magical folklore and fairy tales Lagerlöf's grandmother instilled in her as a child emerge when a stingy shepherd discovers that, upon the arrival of a mysterious visitor, his dogs have suddenly lost their bite and his staff miraculously has a mind of its own!

It was a Christmas Day and all the folks had driven to church except Grandmother and me. We had not been permitted to go along, because one of us was too old and the other was too young. And we were sad, both of us, because we had not been taken to early mass to hear the singing and to see the Christmas candles.

But as we sat there in our loneliness, Grandmother began to tell a story.

"There was a man," said she, "who went out in the dark night to borrow live coals to kindle a fire. He went from hut to hut and knocked. 'Dear friends, help me!' said he. 'My wife has just given birth to a child, and I must make a fire to warm her and the little one.'

"But it was way in the night, and all the people were asleep. No one replied.

"The man walked and walked. At last he saw the gleam of a fire a long way off. Then he went in that direction, and saw that the fire was burning in the open. A lot of sheep were sleeping around the fire, and an old shepherd sat and watched over the flock.

"When the man who wanted to borrow fire came up to the sheep, he saw that three big dogs lay asleep at the shepherd's feet. All three awoke when the man approached and opened their great jaws, as though they wanted to bark; but not a sound was heard. The man noticed that the hair on their backs stood up and that their sharp, white teeth glistened in the firelight. They dashed toward him. He felt that one of them bit at his leg and one at his hand and that one clung to his throat. But their jaws and teeth wouldn't obey them, and the man didn't suffer the least harm.

"Now the man wished to go farther, to get what he needed. But the sheep lay back to back and so close to one another that he couldn't pass them. Then the man stepped upon their backs and walked over them and up to the fire. And not one of the animals awoke or moved.

"When the man had almost reached the fire, the shepherd looked up. He was a surly old man, who was unfriendly and harsh toward human beings. And when he saw the strange man coming, he seized the long spiked staff, which he always held in his hand when he tended his flock, and threw it at him. The staff came right toward the man, but before it reached him, it turned off to one side and whizzed past him, far out in the meadow.

"Now the man came up to the shepherd and said to him: 'Good man, help me, and lend me a little fire! My wife has just given birth to a child, and I must make a fire to warm her and the little one.'

"The shepherd would rather have said no, but when he pondered that the dogs couldn't hurt the man, and the sheep had not run from him, and that the staff had not wished to strike him, he was a little afraid, and dared not deny the man that which he asked.

" 'Take as much as you need!' he said to the man.

"But then the fire was nearly burnt out. There were no logs or branches left, only a big heap of live coals; and the stranger had neither spade nor shovel, wherein he could carry the red-hot coals.

"When the shepherd saw this, he said again: 'Take as much as you need!' And he was glad that the man wouldn't be able to take away any coals.

"But the man stooped and picked coals from the ashes with his bare hands, and laid them in his mantle. And he didn't burn his hands when he touched them, nor did the coals scorch his mantle; but he carried them away as if they had been nuts or apples.

"And when the shepherd, who was such a cruel and hard-hearted man, saw all this, he began to wonder to himself: 'What kind of a night is this, when the dogs do not bite, and sheep are not scared, and the staff does not kill, or the fire scorch?' He called the stranger back, and said to him: 'What

kind of a night is this? And how does it happen that all things show you compassion?'

"Then said the man: 'I cannot tell you if you yourself do not see it.' And he wished to go his way, that he might soon make a fire and warm his wife and child.

"But the shepherd did not wish to lose sight of the man before he had found out what all this might portend. He got up and followed the man till they came to where he lived.

"Then the shepherd saw that the man didn't have so much as a hut to dwell in, but that his wife and babe were lying in a mountain grotto, where there was nothing except the cold and naked stone walls.

"But the shepherd thought that perhaps the poor innocent child might freeze to death there in the grotto; and, although he was a hard man, he was touched, and thought he would like to help it. And he loosened his knapsack from his shoulder, took from it a soft white sheep-skin, gave it to the strange man, and said that he should let the child sleep on it.

"But just as soon as he showed that he, too, could be merciful, his eyes were opened, and he saw what he had not been able to see before and heard what he could not have heard before.

"He saw that all around him stood a ring of little silver-winged angels, and each held a stringed instrument, and all sang in loud tones that tonight the Saviour was born who should redeem the world from its sins.

"Then he understood how all things were so happy this night that they didn't want to do anything wrong.

"And it was not only around the shepherd that there were angels, but he saw them everywhere. They sat inside the grotto, they sat outside on the mountain, and they flew under the heavens. They came marching in great companies, and, as they passed, they cast a glance at the child.

"There was such jubilation and such gladness and songs and play! And all this he saw in the dark night, whereas before he could not have made out anything. He was so happy because his eyes had been opened that he fell upon his knees and thanked God."

Here Grandmother sighed and said: "What that shepherd saw we might also see, for the angels fly down from heaven every Christmas Eve, if we could only see them."

Then Grandmother laid her hand on my head, and said: "You must remember this, for it is as true, as true as that I see you and you see me. It is not revealed by the light of lamps or candles, and it does not depend upon sun and moon; but that which is needful is, that we have such eyes as can see God's glory."

Christmas is coming, the geese are geting fat,
Please to put a penny in the old man's hat;
If you haven't got a penny, a ha'penny will do,
If you haven't got a ha'penny, God bless you!
—BEGGAR'S RHYME

A Christmas Carol
(An Excerpt)

by Charles Dickens

Considered the foremost writer of his time, Charles Dickens had a gift for understanding the nature of people. Born in Portsmouth, England on February 7, 1812, Dickens's family moved to London when he was two. There, he dropped out of school when he was only fourteen, but he used his eye for observation to make up for what he lacked in education when writing his novels.

In the late 1820s, Dickens became a writer for the London Evening Chronicle, *and his first book,* Sketches by Boz, *published in 1836, came from articles he wrote for that newspaper.*

But it was with the publication of The Posthumous Papers of the Pickwick Club, *published in parts in 1836 and 1837, that Dickens became famous. And from that young age of twenty-four, he remained famous until his death from a stroke on June 9, 1870.*

Recognized and revered all over England as well as the United States, Dickens unfortunately was not as successful in his personal life as he was in his professional one. In 1836 he married Catherine Hogarth. But a year later, when Catherine's sister,

Mary, died, Dickens's immense grief over her death led many to believe that it was Mary Hogarth that he actually loved. Nevertheless, Dickens and his wife had ten children before separating in 1858.

A man with enormous energy, Dickens spent his life writing, editing, and touring as a dramatic reader. He also devoted many hours to charities involved with children and the poor, and much of his writing, including his most famous work, A Christmas Carol, was about those less fortunate.

In this excerpt from the timeless story, Ebenezer Scrooge has already been visited by two spirits from his present and past, and he is now about to meet a third spirit from his future. The scariest spirit of them all, the Ghost of Christmas Yet to Come turns the old grouch around, and Scrooge awakens to more than just a beautiful Christmas Day, but also to a future full of love and generosity.

The Phantom slowly, gravely, silently, approached. When it came near him, Scrooge bent down upon his knee, for in the very air through which this Spirit moved it seemed to scatter gloom and mystery.

It was shrouded in a deep black garment, which concealed its head, its face, its form, and left nothing of it visible save one outstretched hand. But for this it would have been difficult to detach its figure from the night, and separate it from the darkness by which it was surrounded.

It was tall and stately when it came beside him, and its mysterious presence filled him with a solemn dread. He knew no more, for the Spirit neither spoke nor moved.

"I am in the presence of the Ghost of Christmas Yet to Come?" said Scrooge.

The Spirit answered not, but pointed onward.

"You are about to show me shadows of the things that have not happened, but will happen in the time before us," Scrooge pursued. "Is that so, Spirit?"

The upper portion of the garment was contracted for an instant in its folds, as if the Spirit had inclined its head. That was the only answer he received.

Although well used to ghostly company by this time, Scrooge feared the silent shape so much that his legs trembled beneath him, and he found that he could hardly stand when he prepared to follow it. The Spirit paused, as if observing his condition, and giving him time to recover.

But Scrooge was all the worse for this. It thrilled him with a vague uncertain horror, to know that, behind the dusky shroud, there were ghostly eyes intently fixed upon him, while he, though he stretched his own to the utmost, could see nothing but a spectral hand and one great heap of black.

"Ghost of the Future!" he exclaimed, "I fear you more than any specter I have seen. But as I know your purpose is to do me good, and as I hope to live to be another man from what I was, I am prepared to bear you company, and do it with a thankful heart. Will you not speak to me?"

It gave him no reply. The hand was pointed straight before them.

"Lead on!" said Scrooge—"lead on! The night is waning fast, and it is precious time to me, I know. Lead on, Spirit!"

The Phantom moved away as it had come toward him. Scrooge followed in the shadow of its dress, which bore him up, he thought, and carried him along.

They scarcely seemed to enter the City, for the City rather seemed to spring up about them, and encompass them of its own act. But there they were, in the heart of it, among the merchants, who hurried up and down, and chinked the money in their pockets, and conversed in groups, and looked at their watches, and trifled thoughtfully with their great gold seals, and so forth, as Scrooge had seen them often.

The Spirit stopped beside one little knot of business men. Observing that the hand was pointed to them, Scrooge advanced to listen to their talk.

"No," said a great fat man with a monstrous chin. "I don't know much about it either way. I only know he's dead."

"When did he die?" inquired another.

"Last night, I believe."

"Why, what was the matter with him?" asked a third, taking a vast quantity of snuff out of a very large snuff-box. "I thought he'd never die."

"God knows," said the first, with a yawn.

"What has he done with his money?" asked a redfaced gentleman with a pendulous excrescence on the end of his nose, that shook like the gills of a turkey.

"I haven't heard," said the man with the large chin, yawning again. "Left it to his company, perhaps. He hasn't left it to *me*. That's all I know."

This pleasantry was received with a general laugh.

"It's likely to be a very cheap funeral," said the same speaker, "for, upon my life, I don't know of anybody to go to it. Suppose we make up a party, and volunteer?"

"I don't mind going if a lunch is provided," observed the gentleman with the excrescence on his nose. "But I must be fed, if I make one."

Another laugh.

"Well, I am the most disinterested among you, after all," said the first speaker, "for I never wear black gloves, and I never eat lunch. But I'll offer to go, if anybody else will. When I come to think of it, I'm not at all sure that I wasn't his most particular friend, for we used to stop and speak whenever we met. By-by!"

Speakers and listeners strolled away, and mixed with other groups. Scrooge knew the men, and looked toward the Spirit for an explanation.

The Phantom glided on into a street. Its finger pointed to two persons meeting.

Scrooge listened again, thinking that the explanation might lie here.

He knew these men, also, perfectly. They were men of business, very wealthy, and of great importance. He had made a point always of standing well in their esteem—that is, strictly in a business point of view.

"How are you?" said one.

"How are you?" returned the other.

"Well!" said the first. "Old Scratch has got his own at last, hey?"

"So I am told," returned the second. "Cold, isn't it?"

"Seasonable for Christmas-time. You are not a skater, I suppose?"

"No. No. Something else to think of. Good morning!"

Not another word. That was their meeting, their conversation, and their parting.

Scrooge was at first inclined to be surprised that the Spirit should attach importance to conversations apparently so trivial, but feeling assured that they must have some hidden purpose, he set himself to consider what it was likely to be. They could scarcely be supposed to have any bearing on the death of Jacob, his old partner, for that was Past, and this Ghost's province was the Future. Nor could he think of any one immediately connected with himself, to whom he could apply them.

But nothing doubting that, to whomsoever they applied, they had some latent moral for his own improvement, he resolved to treasure up every word he heard, and everything he saw, and especially to observe the shadow of himself when it appeared. For he had an expectation that the conduct of his future self would give him the clue he missed, and would render the solution of these riddles easy.

He looked about in that very place for his own image, but another man stood in his accustomed corner, and though the clock pointed to his usual time of day for being there, he saw no likeness of himself among the multitudes that poured in through the Porch.

It gave him little surprise, however, for he had been revolving in his mind a change of life, and thought and hoped he saw his newborn resolutions carried out in this.

Quiet and dark, beside him stood the Phantom, with its outstretched hand. When he roused himself from his thoughtful quest, he fancied, from the turn of the hand and its situation in reference to himself, that the Unseen Eyes were looking at him keenly. It made him shudder, and feel very cold.

They left the busy scene, and went into an obscure part of the town, where Scrooge had never penetrated before, although he recognized its situation, and its bad repute. The ways were foul and narrow, the shops and houses wretched, the people half naked, drunken, slipshod, ugly. Alleys and archways, like so many cesspools, disgorged their offenses of smell, and dirt, and life, upon the straggling streets; and the whole quarter reeked with crime, with filth and misery.

Far in this den of infamous resort, there was a lowbrowed, beetling shop, below a pent-house roof, where iron, old rags, bottles, bones, and greasy offal were bought. Upon the floor within were piled up heaps of rusty keys, nails, chains, hinges, files, scales, weights, and refuse iron of all kinds. Secrets that few would like to scrutinize were bred and hidden in mountains of unseemly rags, masses of corrupted fat, and sepulchers of bones.

Sitting in among the wares he dealt in, by a charcoal stove, made of old bricks, was a grayhaired rascal, nearly seventy years of age, who had screened himself from the cold air without by a frowzy curtaining of miscellaneous tatters, hung upon a line, and smoked his pipe in all the luxury of calm retirement.

Scrooge and the Phantom came into the presence of this man, just as a woman with a heavy bundle slunk into the shop. But she had scarcely entered, when another woman, similarly laden, came in too, and she was closely followed by a man in faded black, who was no less startled by the sight of them than they had been upon the recognition of each other. After a period of blank astonishment, in which the old man with the pipe had joined them, they all three burst into a laugh.

"Let the charwoman alone to be the first!" cried she who had entered first. "Let the laundress alone to be the second, and let the undertaker's man alone to be the third. Look here, old Joe, here's a chance! If we haven't all three met here without meaning it!"

"You couldn't have met in a better place," said old Joe, removing his pipe from his mouth. "Come into the parlor. You were made free of it long ago, you know, and the other two ain't strangers. Stop till I shut the door of the shop. Ah! How it skreeks! There ain't such a rusty bit of metal in the place as its own hinges, I believe, and I'm sure there's no such old bones here as mine. Ha, ha! We're all suitable to our calling, we're well matched. Come into the parlor. Come into the parlor."

The parlor was the space behind the screen of rags. The old man raked the fire together with an old stair-rod, and having trimmed his smoky lamp (for it was night) with the stem of his pipe, put it in his mouth again.

While he did this, the woman who had already spoken threw her bundle on the floor, and sat down in a flaunting manner on a stool, crossing her elbows on her knees, and looking with a bold defiance at the other two.

"What odds, then? What odds, Mrs. Dilber?" said the woman. "Every person has a right to take care of themselves. *He* always did!"

"That's true, indeed!" said the laundress. "No man more so."

"Why, then, don't stand staring as if you was afraid, woman! Who's the wiser? We're not going to pick holes in each other's coats, I suppose?"

"No, indeed!" said Mrs. Dilber and the man together.

"Very well, then!" cried the woman. "That's enough. Who's the worse for the loss of a few things like these? Not a dead man, I suppose?"

"No, indeed," said Mrs. Dilber, laughing.

"If he wanted to keep 'em after he was dead, a wicked old screw," pursued the woman, "why wasn't he natural in his lifetime? If he had been, he'd have had somebody to look after him when he was struck with Death, instead of lying gasping out his last there, alone by himself."

"It's the truest word that ever was spoke," said Mrs. Dilber. "It's a judgment on him."

"I wish it was a little heavier judgment," replied the woman, "and it should have been, you may depend upon it, if I could have laid my hands on anything else. Open that bundle, old Joe, and let me know the value of it. Speak out plain. I'm not afraid to be the first, nor afraid for them to see it. We knew pretty well that we were helping ourselves, before we met here, I believe. It's no sin. Open the bundle."

But the gallantry of her friends would not allow of this, and the man in faded black, mounting the breach first, produced *his* plunder. It was not extensive. A seal or two, a pencil-case, a pair of sleeve-buttons, and a brooch of no great value, were all. They were severally examined and appraised by old Joe, who chalked the sums he was disposed to give for each upon the wall, and added them up into a total when he found that there was nothing more to come.

"That's your account," said Joe, "and I wouldn't give another sixpence, if I was to be boiled. Who's next?"

Mrs. Dilber was next. Sheets and towels, a little wearing-apparel, two old-fashioned silver teaspoons, a pair of sugar-tongs, and a few boots. Her account was stated on the wall in the same manner.

"I always give too much to ladies. It's a weakness of mine, and that's the way I ruin myself," said old Joe. "That's your account. If you asked me for another penny, and made it an open question, I'd repent of being so liberal, and knock off half a crown."

"And now undo my bundle, Joe," said the first woman.

Joe went down on his knees for the greater convenience of opening it, and, having unfastened a great many knots, dragged out a large, heavy roll of some dark stuff.

"What do you call this?" said Joe. "Bed-curtains?"

"Ah!" returned the woman, laughing and leaning forward on her crossed arms. "Bed-curtains!"

"You don't mean to say you took 'em down, rings and all, with him lying there?" said Joe.

"Yes, I do," replied the woman. "Why not?"

"You were born to make your fortune," said Joe, "and you'll certainly do it."

"I certainly sha'n't hold my hand, when I can get anything in it by reaching out, for the sake of such a man as He was, I promise you, Joe," returned the woman coolly. "Don't drop that oil upon the blankets now."

"His blankets?" asked Joe.

"Whose else's do you think?" replied the woman. "He isn't likely to take cold without 'em, I dare say."

"I hope he didn't die of anything catching? Eh?" said old Joe, stopping in his work, and looking up.

"Don't be afraid of that," returned the woman. "I ain't so fond of his company that I'd loiter about him for such things, if he did. Ah! You may look through that shirt till your eyes ache; but you won't find a hole in it, nor a threadbare place. It's the best he had, and a fine one too. They'd have wasted it, if it hadn't been for me."

"What do you call wasting of it?" asked old Joe.

"Putting it on him to be buried in, to be sure," replied the woman, with a laugh. "Somebody was fool enough to do it, but I took it off again. If calico ain't good enough for such a purpose, it isn't good enough for anything. It's quite as becoming to the body. He can't look uglier than he did in that one."

Scrooge listened to this dialogue in horror. As they sat grouped about their spoil, in the scanty light afforded by the old man's lamp, he viewed them with a detestation and disgust which could hardly have been greater though they had been obscene demons, marketing the corpse itself.

"Ha, ha!" laughed the same woman, when old Joe, producing a flannel bag with money in it, told out their several gains upon the ground. "This is the end of it, you see! He frightened every one away from him when he was alive, to profit us when he was dead! Ha, ha, ha!"

"Spirit!" said Scrooge, shuddering from head to foot. "I see, I see. The case of this unhappy man might be my own. My life tends that way now. Merciful Heaven, what is this?"

He recoiled in terror, for the scene had changed, and now he almost touched a bed—a bare, uncurtained bed, on which, beneath a ragged sheet, there lay a something covered up, which, though it was dumb, announced itself in awful language.

The room was very dark, too dark to be observed with any accuracy, though Scrooge glanced round it in obedience to a secret impulse, anxious to know what kind of room it was. A pale light, rising in the outer air, fell straight upon the bed, and on it, plundered and bereft, unwatched, unwept, uncared for, was the body of this man.

Scrooge glanced toward the Phantom. Its steady hand was pointed to the head. The cover was so carelessly adjusted that the slightest raising of it, the motion of a finger upon Scrooge's part, would have disclosed the face. He thought of it, felt how easy it would be to do, and longed to do it, but had no more power to withdraw the veil than to dismiss the specter at his side.

Oh cold, cold, rigid, dreadful Death, set up shine altar here, and dress it with such terrors as thou hast at thy command, for this is thy dominion! But of the loved, revered, and honored head, thou canst not turn one hair to thy dread purposes, or make one feature odious. It is not that the hand is heavy, and will fall down when released; it is not that the heart and pulse are still: but that the hand was open, generous, and true, the heart brave, warm, and tender, and the pulse a man's. Strike, Shadow, strike! And see his good deeds springing from the wound, to sow the world with life immortal!

No voice pronounced these words in Scrooge's ears, and yet he heard them when he looked upon the bed. He thought, if this man could be raised up now, what would be his foremost thoughts? Avarice, hard dealing, griping cares? They have brought him to a rich end, truly!

He lay, in the dark, empty house, with not a man, a woman, or a child to say he was kind to me in this or that, and for the memory of one kind word I will be kind to him. A cat was tearing at the door, and there was a sound of gnawing rats beneath the hearthstone. What *they* wanted in the room of death, and why they were so restless and disturbed, Scrooge did not dare to think.

"Spirit!" he said, "this is a fearful place. In leaving it, I shall not leave its lesson, trust me. Let us go!"

Still the Ghost pointed with an unmoved finger.

"I understand you," Scrooge returned, "and I would do it, if I could. But I have not the power, Spirit."

Again it seemed to look upon him.

"If there is any person in the town who feels emotion caused by this man's death," said Scrooge, quite agonized, "show that person to me, Spirit, I beseech you!"

The Phantom spread its dark robe before him for a moment, like a wing and withdrawing it, revealed a room by daylight, where a mother and her children were.

She was expecting some one, and with anxious eagerness: for she walked up and down the room, started at every sound, looked out from the window, glanced at the clock, tried, but in vain, to work with her needle, and could hardly bear the voices of her children in their play.

At length the long-expected knock was heard. She hurried to the door, and met her husband, a man whose face was care-worn and depressed, though he was young. There was a remarkable expression in it now, a kind of serious delight of which he felt ashamed, and which he struggled to repress.

He sat down to the dinner that had been hoarding for him by the fire, and when she asked him faintly what news (which was not until after a long silence), he appeared embarrassed how to answer.

"Is it good," she said, "or bad?"—to help him.

"Bad," he answered.

"We are quite ruined?"

"No. There is hope yet, Caroline."

"If *he* relents," she said, amazed, "there is! Nothing is past hope, if such a miracle has happened."

"He is past relenting," said her husband. "He is dead."

She was a mild and patient creature, if her face spoke truth; but she was thankful in her soul to hear it, and she said so, with clasped hands.

She prayed forgiveness the next moment, and was sorry, but the first was the emotion of her heart.

"What the half-drunken woman whom I told you of last night said to me, when I tried to see him and obtain a week's delay, and what I thought was a mere excuse to avoid me, turns out to have been quite true. He was not only very ill, but dying, then."

"To whom will our debt be transferred?"

"I don't know. But before that time we shall be ready with the money and even though we were not, it would be bad fortune indeed to find so merciless a creditor in his successor. We may sleep tonight with light hearts, Caroline!"

Yes. Soften it as they would, their hearts were lighter. The children's faces, hushed and clustered round to hear what they so little understood, were brighter, and it was a happier house for this man's death! The only emotion that the Ghost could show him, caused by the event, was one of pleasure.

"Let me see some tenderness connected with a death," said Scrooge, "or that dark chamber, Spirit, which we left just now will be forever present to me."

The Ghost conducted him through several streets familiar to his feet and, as they went along, Scrooge looked here and there to find himself, but nowhere was he to be seen. They entered poor Bob Cratchit's house—the dwelling he had visited before—and found the mother and children seated round the fire.

Quiet. Very quiet.

The noisy little Cratchits were as still as statues in one corner, and sat looking up at Peter, who had a book before him. The mother and her daughters were engaged in sewing. But surely they were very quiet!

"'And he took a child, and set him in the midst of them.'"

Where had Scrooge heard those words? He had not dreamed them. The boy must have read them out, as he and the Spirit crossed the threshold. Why did he not go on?

The mother laid her work upon the table, and put her hand up to her face.

"The color hurts my eyes," she said.

The color? Ah, poor Tiny Tim!

"They're better now again," said Cratchit's wife. "It makes them weak by candle-light; and I wouldn't show weak eyes to your father when he comes home, for the world. It must be near his time."

"Past it, rather," Peter answered, shutting up his book. "But I think he has walked a little slower than he used, these few last evenings, mother."

They were very quiet again. At last she said, and in a steady, cheerful voice, that only faltered once:

"I have known him walk with—I have known him walk with Tiny Tim upon his shoulder very fast indeed."

"And so have I," cried Peter. "Often."

"And so have I," exclaimed another. So had all.

"But he was very light to carry," she resumed, intent upon her work, "and his father loved him so, that it was no trouble—no trouble. And there is your father at the door!"

She hurried out to meet him, and little Bob in his comforter—he had need of it, poor fellow—came in. His tea was ready for him on the hob, and, they all tried who should help him to it most.

Then the two young Cratchits got upon his knees, and laid, each child, a little cheek against his face, as if they said, "Don't mind it, father. Don't be grieved!"

Bob was very cheerful with them, and spoke pleasantly to all the family. He looked at the work upon the table, and praised the industry and speed of Mrs. Cratchit and the girls. They would be done long before Sunday, he said.

"Sunday! You went to-day, then, Robert?" said his wife.

"Yes, my dear," returned Bob. "I wish you could have gone. It would have done you good to see how green a place it is. But you'll see it often. I promised him that I would walk there on a Sunday. My little, little child!" cried Bob.

He broke down all at once. He couldn't help it. If he could have helped it, he and his child would have been farther apart, perhaps, than they were.

He left the room, and went up-stairs into the room above, which was lighted cheerfully, and hung with Christmas. There was a chair set close beside the child, and there were signs of some one having been there lately. Poor Bob sat down in it, and when he had thought a little and composed himself, he kissed the little face. He was reconciled to what had happened, and went down again quite happy.

They drew about the fire and talked, the girls and mother working still. Bob told them of the extraordinary kindness of Mr. Scrooge's nephew, whom he had scarcely seen but once, and who, meeting him in the street that day, and seeing that he looked a little—"just a little down, you know," said Bob, inquired what had happened to distress him. "On which," said Bob, "for he is the pleasantest-spoken gentleman you ever heard, I told him. 'I am heartily sorry for it, Mr. Cratchit,' he said, 'and heartily sorry for your good wife.' By the by, how he ever knew *that*, I don't know."

"Knew what, my dear?"

"Why, that you were a good wife," replied Bob.

"Everybody knows that," said Peter.

"Very well observed, my boy!" cried Bob. "I hope they do. 'Heartily sorry,' he said, 'for your good wife. If I can be of service to you in any way,' he said, giving me his card, 'that's where I live. Pray come to me.' Now it wasn't," cried Bob, "for the sake of anything he might be able to do for us, so much as for his kind way, that this was quite delightful. It really seemed as if he had known our Tiny Tim, and felt with us."

"I'm sure he's a good soul!" said Mrs. Cratchit.

"You would be sure of it, my dear," returned Bob, "if you saw and spoke to him. I shouldn't be at all surprised—mark what I say!—if he got Peter a better situation."

"Only hear that, Peter," said Mrs. Cratchit.

"And then," cried one of the girls, "Peter will be keeping company with some one, and setting up for himself."

"Get along with you!" retorted Peter, grinning.

"It's just as likely as not," said Bob, "one of these days, though there's plenty of time for that, my dear. But, however and whenever we part from one another, I am sure we shall not forget poor Tiny Tim—shall we?—or this first parting that there was among us?"

"Never, father!" cried they all.

"And I know," said Bob—"I know, my dears, that when we recollect how patient and how mild he was, although he was a little, little child, we shall not quarrel easily among ourselves, and forget poor Tiny Tim in doing it."

"No, never, father!" they all cried again.

"I am very happy," said little Bob—"I am very happy!"

Mrs. Cratchit kissed him, his daughters kissed him, the two young Cratchits kissed him, and Peter and himself shook hands. Spirit of Tiny Tim, thy essence was from God!

"Specter," said Scrooge, "something informs me that our parting moment is at hand. I know it, but I know not how. Tell me what man that was whom we saw lying dead."

The Ghost of Christmas Yet to Come conveyed him, as before—though at a different time, he thought; indeed, there seemed no order in these latter visions, save that they were in the Future—into the resorts of business men, but showed him not himself.

Indeed, the Spirit did not stay for anything, but went straight on, as to the end just now desired, until besought by Scrooge to tarry for a moment.

"This court," said Scrooge, "through which we hurry now is where my place of occupation is, and has been for a length of time. I see the house. Let me behold what I shall be, in days to come!"

The Spirit stopped; the hand was pointed elsewhere.

"The house is yonder," Scrooge exclaimed. "Why do you point away?"

The inexorable finger underwent no change.

Scrooge hastened to the window of his office, and looked in. It was an office still, but not his. The furniture was not the same, and the figure in the chair was not himself. The Phantom pointed as before.

He joined it once again, and, wondering why and whither he had gone, accompanied it until they reached an iron gate. He paused to look round before entering.

A churchyard. Here, then, the wretched man whose name he had now to learn lay underneath the ground. It was a worthy place. Walled in by houses, overrun by grass and weeds, the growth of vegetation's death, not life; choked up with too much burying, fat with repleted appetite.

The Spirit stood among the graves, and pointed down to One. He advanced toward it, trembling. The Phantom was exactly as it had been, but he dreaded that he saw new meaning in its solemn shape.

"Before I draw nearer to that stone to which you point," said Scrooge, "answer me one question. Are these the shadows of the things that Will be or are they shadows of the things that May be, only?"

Still the Ghost pointed downward to the grave by which it stood.

"Men's courses will foreshadow certain ends, to which, if persevered in, they must lead," said Scrooge. "But if the courses be departed from, the ends will change. Say it is thus with what you show me!"

The Spirit was immovable as ever.

Scrooge crept toward it, trembling as he went; and following the finger, read upon the stone of the neglected grave his own name, EBENEZER SCROOGE.

"Am *I* that man who lay upon the bed," he cried, upon his knees.

The finger pointed from the grave to him, and back again.

"No, Spirit! Oh, no, no!"

The finger still was there.

"Spirit!" he cried, tightly clutching at its robe, "Hear me! I am not the man I was. I will not be the man I must have been. Why show me this, if I am past all hope?"

For the first time the hand appeared to shake.

"Good Spirit," he pursued, as down upon the ground he fell before it, "your nature intercedes for me, and pities me. Assure me that I yet may change these shadows you have shown me, by an altered life!"

The kind hand trembled.

"I will honor Christmas in my heart, and try to keep it all the year. I will live in the Past, Present, and the Future. The Spirits of all Three shall strive within me. I will not shut out the lessons that they teach. Oh, tell me I may sponge away the writing on this stone!"

In his agony he caught the spectral hand. It sought to free itself, but he was strong in his entreaty, and detained it. The Spirit, stronger yet, repulsed him.

Holding up his hands in a last prayer to have his fate reversed, he saw an alteration in the Phantom's hood and dress. It shrunk, collapsed, and dwindled down into a bedpost.

Yes! and the bedpost was his own. The bed was his own, the room was his own. Best and happiest of all, the Time before him was his own, to make amends in!

"I will live in the Past, the Present, and the Future!" Scrooge repeated as he scrambled out of bed. "The Spirits of all Three shall strive within me. Oh Jacob Marley! Heaven and the Christmas Time be praised for this! I say it on my knees, old Jacob; on my knees!"

He was so fluttered and so glowing with his good intentions, that his broken voice would scarcely answer to his call. He had been sobbing violently in his conflict with the Spirit, and his face was wet with tears.

"They are not torn down," cried Scrooge, folding one of his bed-curtains in his arms. "They are not torn down, rings and all. They are here; I am here; the shadows of the things that would have been may be dispelled. They will be. I know they will!"

His hands were busy with his garments all this time: turning them inside out, putting them on upside down, tearing them, mislaying them, making them parties to every kind of extravagance.

"I don't know what to do!" cried Scrooge, laughing and crying in the same breath, and making a perfect Laocoön of himself with his stockings. "I am as light as a feather, I am as happy as an angel, I am as merry as a schoolboy, I am as giddy as a drunken man. A merry Christmas to everybody! A happy New Year to all the world! Hallo there! Whoop! Hallo!"

He had frisked into the sitting-room, and was now standing there, perfectly winded.

"There's the saucepan that the gruel was in!" cried Scrooge, starting off again, and going round the fireplace. "There's the door by which the Ghost of Jacob Marley entered! There's the corner where the Ghost of Christmas Present sat! There's the window where I saw the wandering Spirits! It's all right, it's all true, it all happened. Ha, ha, ha!"

Really, for a man who had been out of practice for so many years, it was a splendid laugh, a most illustrious laugh. The father of a long, long line of brilliant laughs!

"I don't know what day of the month it is!" said Scrooge. "I don't know how long I've been among the Spirits. I don't know anything. I'm quite a baby. Never mind. I don't care. I'd rather be a baby. Hallo! Whoop! Hallo here!"

He was checked in his transports by the churches ringing out the lustiest peals he had ever heard. Clash, clash, hammer; ding, dong, bell! Bell, dong, ding; hammer, clash, clash! Oh, glorious, glorious!

Running to the window, he opened it, and put out his head. No fog, no mist; clear, bright, jovial, stirring, cold; cold, piping for the blood to dance to; golden sunlight; heavenly sky; sweet fresh air; merry bells. Oh, glorious! Glorious!

"What's today?" cried Scrooge, calling downward to a boy in Sunday clothes, who perhaps had loitered in to look.

"Eh?" returned the boy with all his might of wonder.

"What's today, my fine fellow?" said Scrooge.

"Today!" replied the boy. "Why, Christmas Day."

"It's Christmas Day!" said Scrooge to himself. "I haven't missed it. The Spirits have done it all in one night. They can do anything they like. Of course they can. Of course they can. Hallo, my fine fellow!"

"Hallo!" returned the boy.

"Do you know the poulterer's in the next street but one, at the corner?" Scrooge inquired.

"I should hope I did," replied the lad.

"An intelligent boy!" cried Scrooge. "A remarkable boy! Do you know whether they've sold the prize turkey that was hanging up there? Not the little prize turkey: the big one?"

"What? the one as big as me?" returned the boy.

"What a delightful boy!" said Scrooge. "It's a pleasure to talk to him. Yes, my buck!"

"It's hanging there now," replied the boy.

"Is it?" said Scrooge. "Go and buy it."

"Walk-ER!" exclaimed the boy.

"No, no," said Scrooge, "I am in earnest. Go and buy it, and tell 'em to bring it here, that I may give them the directions where to take it. Come back with the man, and I'll

give you a shilling. Come back with him in less than five minutes, and I'll give you half-a-crown!"

The boy was off like a shot. He must have had a steady hand at a trigger who could have got a shot off half as fast.

"I'll send it to Bob Cratchit's," whispered Scrooge, rubbing his hands, and splitting with a laugh. "He shan't know who sends it. It's twice the size of Tiny Tim. Joe Miller never made such a joke as sending it to Bob's will be!"

The hand in which he wrote the address was not a steady one; but write it he did, somehow, and went downstairs to open the street door, ready for the coming of the poulterer's man. As he stood there, waiting his arrival, the knocker caught his eye.

"I shall love it as long as I live!" cried Scrooge patting it with his hand. "I scarcely ever looked at it before. What an honest expression it has in its face! It's a wonderful knocker!—Here's the turkey. Hallo! Whoop! How are you! Merry Christmas!"

It was a turkey! He never could have stood upon his legs, that bird. He would have snapped 'em short off in a minute, like sticks of sealing-wax.

"Why, it's impossible to carry that to Camden Town," said Scrooge. "You must have a cab."

The chuckle with which he said this, and the chuckle with which he paid for the turkey, and the chuckle with which he paid for the cab, and the chuckle with which he recompensed the boy, were only to be exceeded by the chuckle with which he sat down breathless in his chair again, and chuckled until he cried.

Shaving was not an easy task, for his hand continued to shake very much; and shaving requires attention, even when you don't dance while you are at it. But if he had cut the end of his nose off, he would have put a piece of sticking-plaster over it, and been quite satisfied.

He dressed himself "all in his best," and at last got out into the streets. The people were by this time pouring forth, as he had seen them with the Ghost of Christmas Present; and walking with his hands behind him, Scrooge regarded every one with a delighted smile.

He looked so irresistibly pleasant, in a word, that three or four good-humored fellows said, "Good morning, sir! A merry Christmas to you!" And Scrooge said often afterward that, of all the blithe sounds he had ever heard, those were the blithest in his ears.

He had not gone far when, coming on toward him, he beheld the portly gentleman who had walked into his counting-house the day before and said, "Scrooge and Marley's, I believe?" It sent a pang across his heart to think how this old gentleman would look upon him when they met; but he knew what path lay straight before him, and he took it.

"My dear sir," said Scrooge, quickening his pace, and taking the old gentleman by both his hands, "how do you do? I hope you succeeded yesterday. It was very kind of you. A merry Christmas to you, sir!"

"Mr. Scrooge?"

"Yes," said Scrooge. "That is my name, and I fear that it may not be pleasant to you. Allow me to ask your pardon. And will you have the goodness—" here Scrooge whispered in his ear.

"Lord bless me!" cried the gentleman, as if his breath were taken away. "My dear Mr. Scrooge, are you serious?"

"If you please," said Scrooge. "Not a farthing less. A great many back-payments are included in it, I assure you. Will you do me that favor?"

"My dear sir," said the other, shaking hands with him, "I don't know what to say to such munifi—"

"Don't say anything, please," retorted Scrooge. "Come and see me. Will you come and see me?"

"I will!" cried the old gentleman. And it was clear he meant to do it.

"Thankee," said Scrooge. "I am much obliged to you. I thank you fifty times. Bless you!"

He went to the church, and walked about the streets, and watched the people hurrying to and fro, and patted the children on the head, and questioned beggars, and looked down into the kitchens of houses, and up to the windows; and found that everything could yield him pleasure. He had never dreamed that any walk—that anything—could give him so much happiness. In the afternoon he turned his steps toward his nephew's house.

He passed the door a dozen times before he had the courage to go up and knock. But he made a dash and did it.

"Is your master at home, my dear?" said Scrooge to the girl. "Nice girl! Very."

"Yes, sir."

"Where is he, my love?" said Scrooge.

"He's in the dining-room, sir, along with the mistress. I'll show you upstairs, if you please."

"Thankee. He knows me," said Scrooge, with his hand already on the dining-room lock. "I'll go in here, my dear."

He turned it gently, and sidled his face in round the door. They were looking at the table (spread out in great array); for these young housekeepers are always nervous on such points, and like to see that everything is right.

"Fred!" said Scrooge.

Dear heart alive, how his niece by marriage started! Scrooge had forgotten, for the moment, about her sitting in the corner with the footstool, or he wouldn't have done it on any account.

"Why, bless my soul!" cried Fred, "who's that?"

"It's I. You uncle Scrooge. I have come to dinner. Will you let me in, Fred?"

Let him in! It is a mercy he didn't shake his arm off. He was at home in five minutes. Nothing could be heartier. His niece looked just the same. So did Topper when he came. So did the plump sister when she came. So did every one when they came. Wonderful party, wonderful games, wonderful unanimity, won-der-ful happiness!

But he was early at the office next morning. Oh, he was early there! If he could only be there first, and catch Bob Cratchit coming late!

That was the thing he had set his heart upon.

And he did it; yes, he did! The clock struck nine. No Bob. A quarter past. No Bob. He was a full eighteen minutes and a half behind his time. Scrooge sat with his door wide open, that he might see him come into the tank.

His hat was off before he opened the door; his comforter too. He was on his stool in a jiffy, driving away with his pen, as if he were trying to overtake nine o'clock.

"Hallo!" growled Scrooge in his accustomed voice as near as he could feign it. "What do you mean by coming here at this time of day?"

"I am very sorry, sir," said Bob, "I am behind my time."

"You are?" repeated Scrooge. "Yes, I think you are. Step this way, sir, if you please."

"It's only once a year, sir," pleaded Bob, appearing from the tank. "It shall not be repeated. I was making rather merry yesterday, sir."

"Now, I'll tell you what, my friend," said Scrooge, "I am not going to stand this sort of thing any longer. And therefore," he continued, leaping from his stool, and giving Bob such a dig in the waistcoat that he staggered back into the tank again—"I am about to raise your salary!"

Bob trembled, and got a little nearer to the ruler. He had a momentary idea of knocking Scrooge down with it, holding him, and calling to the people in the court for help and a strait-waistcoat.

"A merry Christmas, Bob!" said Scrooge, with an earnestness that could not be mistaken, as he clapped him on the back. "A merrier Christmas, Bob, my good fellow, than I have given you for many a year! I'll raise your salary, and endeavor to assist your struggling family, and we will discuss your affairs this very afternoon, over a Christmas bowl of smoking bishop, Bob! Make up the fires and buy another coal-scuttle before you dot another i, Bob Cratchit!"

Scrooge was better than his word. He did it all, and infinitely more; and to Tiny Tim, who did NOT die, he was a second father. He became as good a friend, as good a master, and as good a man as the good old city knew, or any other good old city, town, or borough in the good old world. Some people laughed to see the alteration in him, but he let them laugh, and little heeded them; for he was wise enough to know that nothing ever happened on this globe, for good, at which some people did not have their fill of laughter at the outset; and knowing that such as these would be blind anyway, he thought it quite as well that they should wrinkle up their eyes in grins as have the malady in less attractive forms. His own heart laughed, and that was quite enough for him.

He had no further dialogue with Spirits, but lived upon the Total Abstinence Principle ever afterward; and it was always said of him that he knew how to keep Christmas well, if any man alive possessed the knowledge. May that be truly said of us, and all of us! And so, as Tiny Tim observed, God Bless Us, Every One!

At Christmas play and make good cheer,
For Chirstmas comes but once a year.
　　　　　　　　　　—THOMAS TUSSER,
A Hundred Good Points of Husbandry [1557]
The Farmer's Daily Diet

Glossary

abashed to make embarrassed or ashamed

bliss supreme happiness; heaven, paradise

bourn destination; domain

brethren male members, as of a congregation or fraternal organization; fellow members

brindled gray or tawny with darker streaks or spots

chilblains sore caused by exposure to the cold

corsair a fast ship used for piracy

courser a swift horse

dogmas established beliefs or principles

duplicity deceitfulness in speech or behavior; double-dealing

forsooth in truth; in fact; indeed

gamboled to skip about, as in dancing or playing

grotto cave or cavern

heretical characteristic of one who opposes an established view or principle

hob a projection in the fireplace where things are kept warm

impertinent rude

impetuously acting rashly, without thought

injunction a command or order

insurrection an act of rising in arms or open rebellion against an established authority

libel anything that maliciously misrepresents or damages a reputation

lustre radiant or luminous brightness; brilliance

marrowfat pea a large-seeded variety of pea

mooted doubtful; debatable

ogress a monstrously ugly, cruel, barbarous woman

palpable readily or plainly seen; obvious

pâté de foie gras a spread made of finely chopped or pureed goose liver

portend to indicate in advance, as an omen

reprehended to have found fault with

rife abundant, plentiful, or numerous

sagacious shrewd, wise

scanty insufficient in amount, extent, or degree

servile characteristic of, proper to, or customary for slaves

smitten impressed favorably; charmed

strenuous intensively active; vigorous

strychnine a colorless, crystalline poison

twinkling the time required for a wink; an instant

viand an article of food